PRAISE FOR STEENA HOLMES

"Steena Holmes is a natural storyteller who skillfully aims for the heart--and writes from it too."
– C.J. Carmichael, national bestselling author of *The Fourth Child*.

"In *The Memory Child*, Steena Holmes explores motherhood, love, and the notion of who we really are, all of which adds up to a complex, character-driven story that packs a great punch."
—llison Winn Scotch, *New York Times* bestselling author of *Time of My Life* and *The Theory of Opposites*

"Poignant and richly drawn, Steena Holmes has created a layered and complex story."
– Jane Porter, bestselling author of *Flirting with Forty* and *Easy on the Eyes*

The
WORD
GAME

Also by Steena Holmes

Finding Emma
Emma's Secret
The Memory Child
Stillwater Rising

The

WORD
GAME

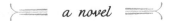 *a novel*

NEW YORK TIMES & USA TODAY BESTSELLING AUTHOR

STEENA HOLMES

LAKE UNION
PUBLISHING

Published by Lake Union, Seattle
www.apub.com

Amazon, the Amazon logo, and Lake Union are trademarks of Amazon.com, Inc., or its affiliates.

ISBN-13: 9781503949430 (hardcover)
ISBN-10: 1503949435 (hardcover)
ISBN-13: 9781503947139 (paperback)
ISBN-10: 1503947130 (paperback)

Cover design by Mumtaz Mustafa
Printed in the United States of America

First Edition

CHAPTER ONE

ALYSON
FRIDAY NIGHT

In this moment, at the core of who she was and all she wanted to be, Alyson Ward was happy. Contented, even—for the first time in years. She didn't understand it, but it was amazing how one simple decision, one act of letting go and giving in, could change so much.

"This is kind of fun, isn't it?" she said.

Rachel, her best friend, raised her glass of merlot in agreement. "Fun? It's brilliant. I'm so glad you thought to do this for the parents. And a chocolate and wine tasting? Great idea. If it had been left up to me, we'd be sitting at the pub right now."

Alyson took a quick sip of wine and looked around the room. The small restaurant was packed with parents and friends from the dance group. Her husband and Rachel's were both at the bar, talking with a few friends.

"I like doing stuff like this. You know that." Alyson settled back in her chair and thought about checking in with her daughter but decided there was no need. If anything happened, her sister would call.

"Maybe consider a second career in event planning? Accountant during the day, event planner by night. Could be a good business." Rachel reached for one of the remaining chocolates from the tasting.

"Ha. I'd be the most frazzled event planner. And you know I like working with numbers." Alyson winked before she reached for her own small piece of dark chocolate.

One of the things taught them by their speaker tonight was how to savor the chocolate—to take small bites, let it sit on the tongue, and allow the flavor to announce itself. If you chew the chocolate too fast, you don't get any of the nuances, and in fact, it can turn out to be quite bitter. Alyson wasn't a fervent chocoholic, but she had to admit, eating it slowly did make a world of difference.

"The kids performed really well tonight, didn't they?" Rachel pulled out her phone and began scrolling through the photos she'd taken of the evening.

The dance recital had been fun, and their girls had done a great job. The styles Myah had incorporated into the routine had been a balanced blend of contemporary and jazz, and considering this had been the first recital for this new class, it'd been a success. To celebrate, all the girls were over at Tricia's house, Alyson's sister, for a sleepover. It would be a madhouse with all those kids, but Tricia no doubt reveled in the chaos. She was like that. Alyson, on the other hand, needed to be in control of things—which is probably why she enjoyed working with numbers and spreadsheets so much. She created order out of disarray for her clients, and loved it.

"Myah did such an amazing job. I was actually surprised at how well it all turned out."

"Maybe if you actually came to more of the classes and rehearsals, you wouldn't have been so surprised."

"Give me a break, Aly. You know my schedule is crazy on the best of days. I try to make as many practices as I can, but honestly, if

I have to sit beside Melinda Brown and listen to her complain about Myah and her class one more time . . ." Rachel sighed and reached for her almost-empty wineglass.

Rachel was the principal of the elementary school and, to be fair, was quite busy with after-school programs and meetings.

"You're right. I'm sorry. I don't blame you about Melinda either. Although, isn't she on the PTA?"

Rachel shook her head. "Not this year. I might have talked her out of running for another year." She looked around to make sure Melinda wasn't within earshot. "But don't tell anyone, because you know I'll have to deny it."

Alyson fiddled with her glass but didn't say anything. They both knew Melinda Brown wasn't one of her favorite people.

"Did you happen to book our next cooking class? I know you were waiting to see about your schedule." It was Rachel's turn to pick the class, their last of the year before things got busy with Christmas concerts and parties.

"How does pizza sound? Apparently, we'll learn from a guest chef from Naples. Just think, real authentic Italian pizza. Oh, that reminds me, I actually have the whole weekend off, so Paul has convinced me to try out a new bed-and-breakfast that one of his friends opened on the coast. He wanted to leave Friday after school, but I told him we had a date. So," she twirled a thick strand of her long hair in her fingers, "do you think Melanie can sleep over on Saturday while we're gone?" Rachel glanced over to where their husbands stood and waved. Her husband blew her a kiss.

Alyson rolled her eyes, but then Rachel elbowed her in the side.

"You guys can be sickening some days. You know that, right? You've been married how long? I swear, at times you still act like newlyweds. And, of course, Melanie can stay over. She's always welcome." Alyson teased her, but she had to admit to being a little jealous at the same time. They both had celebrated their fourteenth wedding anniversary this past year, Alyson in the spring and Rachel in the summer, but that didn't mean their marriages were the same.

For fun, Alyson and Rachel once filled out an online marriage survey and were asked to sum up their marriage in three words. Alyson had used the words *comfortable, stable, secure*. Rachel, on the other hand, listed *passionate, fun, deep*.

"Oh look. It's Debra." Rachel's eyes skimmed the tables, and she waved to someone who sat across the room with a bunch of other women.

"Who's Debra?" Alyson didn't recognize her.

"She's new. Just moved from Boston. She's a social worker and really nice."

Alyson glanced at the woman and forced a smile. She wasn't overly fond of social workers in general—not after having problems with one years ago.

"Alyson! There you are. Why are you hiding away in the corner? And where is Myah? I thought she'd be here by now," said one of the women among the group of other moms surrounding their table, wineglasses in hand. "Whoever came up with the idea of the kids and adults having their separate parties was brilliant. I bet it was you, wasn't it?"

Alyson blushed. "Myah's at Tricia's. She'll be here shortly. It was Tricia's idea actually. She thought it would be a fun way for the kids to celebrate, and then, well, you know how things escalate." Her head dipped toward her tensed shoulders, and she became aware of feeling uncomfortable with everyone looking at her.

"What's she's not saying, Penny"—Rachel leaned forward and rested her elbows on the table—"is that yes, it was her idea for the parents to have their own party, and then she went a step beyond and organized the wine and chocolate tasting with a real Parisian chocolatier."

Alyson sat back and sipped more of her wine as Rachel came to the rescue and took the attention off of her.

"Thank you," Alyson said quietly once Penny and the ladies left and Scott and Paul returned.

"And this is why you're not an event planner." Rachel smiled. "You need to start accepting these accolades you know. You are amazing, and everyone knows it."

"Amazing? My wife? Didn't you know she's secretly Wonder Woman?" Scott scooted in beside her in their booth and placed his arm around her shoulders.

"Stop. Both of you." Alyson's gaze settled on the menu she'd set aside. "Anyone hungry? I'm thinking—"

"A plate of nachos or fried pickles or even a basket of wings sounds good right about now." Scott plucked the menu from her hand and winked at her.

"I'm surprised you didn't suggest the fried calamari too," she teased him.

His eyebrows rose in pretend surprise. "Hey, I plan on taking full advantage of this evening. You do realize that right?"

She chuckled but didn't bother to reply. She made sure they ate clean at home, and while her husband had benefited from their improved diet and lost almost twenty pounds, she knew he still craved all those deep-fried death sentences she refused to allow in the house anymore.

Scott waved a waitress over, and everyone ordered an appetizer to share, even Alyson who got the special hummus and pita plate.

"Did you notice the renovations at the theater? It looks great. Scott, did you guys work on that?" Paul, Rachel's husband, asked. Paul worked as lawyer at one of the firms in their small town.

Scott shrugged. "Eddie didn't think we're specialized enough, so he brought in some city crew that probably cost him a small fortune."

Alyson focused on a water stain on the table. If you can't say something nice, don't say anything at all, right? And when it came to Eddie, Myah's soon-to-be ex-husband, she had absolutely nothing nice to say at all.

"Why would he do that when you probably would have been cheaper?"

"Who knows why that man does a lot of things? No doubt he found someone to sponsor the upgrades in exchange for something else. You know how Eddie works." He drank some of his beer. "Either way though, the place does look great."

Scott worked alongside Alyson's father and Tricia's husband as a carpenter at Wilhem & Sons Designs. They were the go-to carpentry company in town.

"I heard he wants to get back to doing competitions," Rachel said.

Alyson turned. "Who did you hear that from? He'd need a new partner for that, because I know for sure Myah has given up competitive dancing. She's happy teaching now."

"Well, they are separated. Maybe that's his new partner there?" Rachel pointed toward the bar where Eddie stood with his arm around a tall blonde's waist. "Was he even there tonight for Keera?"

"He was. I saw him off to the side giving her a pep talk and hug." Alyson eyed the woman, not recognizing her at all. Why would he bring her here? He knew the dance parents were coming here. He'd gotten the invitation as well, unless . . . he wanted to show everyone that he was moving on from Myah?

"Ignore him. He's here for the attention. You know that." Scott said to her, nudging her knee with his own. "I have to say, I'm impressed." Scott said. He glanced at his watch. "It's been over two hours, and I don't think I've seen you use your phone yet." He leaned over and kissed her on the cheek. "Tell me you haven't called to check in on Lyla."

"I haven't." She smiled back at him with happiness.

"Worried?"

She shook her head. "Not at all."

He arched an eyebrow, as if challenging her to tell him the truth. But she was.

"You were right, and I was wrong. She's almost eleven and probably the only girl in the group who hasn't gone to a sleepover party. It's time." She played with the napkin in her lap, twisting the corners while managing to contain her smile.

She was happy. It *was* time. Time for her to let go of some of her control over her daughter, time for Lyla to grow up and spread her wings a little. And she was at her sister's . . . a place completely safe and trustworthy.

"Anyway, if she gets scared, she can come home." She released the napkin and smoothed it back over her lap.

"But she won't," said Rachel. "She's going to have so much fun with everyone tonight that she won't even think about it being her first real sleepover."

Tonight was a big deal, in more ways than one, and everyone here at the table knew and understood that. By letting Lyla go to the sleepover, it meant Alyson was giving up some of the control she'd held on to so tightly all of her daughter's life. It meant taking a step toward putting her marriage first—the real secret to why Rachel and Paul were still so much in love. It meant learning to trust others as well, like her own husband, who'd been the one to champion the sleepover at Tricia's.

That happiness she'd felt earlier in the evening—it was still there, and she'd ride this wave for as long as possible. After all, her daughter was at her sister's house . . . what could go wrong?

CHAPTER TWO

TRICIA

Amid shrieks and giggles and the sounds of revved-up engines and blowing horns, Tricia laughed. She loved when her house was full of exuberant children and ordered chaos, as if the very energy in the room filled her up.

"Are you sure we don't have room for more kids? We could invite the boys' soccer teams over." Mark joined her at the kitchen table where she sat and clamped his hands over his ears.

"Oh, come on, you love this as much as I do." She beamed a full smile at him and then laughed again at the look on his face. "Okay, maybe not so much the shrieking. Maybe you should go tell the boys to tone it down a little. They're worse than the girls right now."

"Worse than the girls? I'd say they're worse than the dogs." Mark snapped his fingers at the dogs, who immediately sat down and whined. They obviously wanted to join the boys in their fun.

The boys were in the family room playing some car game on the system Mark had connected to the surround sound.

When Tricia had suggested using their home for the dance group's recital sleepover, her three boys had complained about the house being overrun by girls, until she'd suggested they each invite one of their friends to sleep over. Yes, it made things a bit more . . . challenging, having a house full of fifteen children, but what was life without something fun to shake things up?

"Maybe all this sugar so late at night wasn't the best idea?"

Tricia lifted her mug of coffee. "No, but this is." It was after nine, and she was on her second cup and it wasn't decaf. Normally by now, she'd be in bed, cuddled up beside her husband, watching one of their recorded shows. But she had a funny feeling there would be no sleeping or cuddling, or anything else, until the wee hours of the morning.

"When is the pizza coming?"

Mark glanced at his watch. "Anytime now. I ordered extra, knowing what the boys are like. No doubt they'll be sneaking into the kitchen while we're sleeping and raid the fridge."

"There'd better not be any sneaking tonight. Not for food or anything else . . ." Tricia shook her head at the thought. She had a house stuffed full of children ranging from the ages of eight all the way to thirteen, and even though the majority of the kids were girls, she wasn't naïve.

Girls could be the worst culprits when it came to troublemaking.

"Is Myah still here?" Mark eyed the empty cup at the table, where Myah had sat a little while ago.

"She just went out to her car. She brought the girls some party bags to celebrate their first recital and needs to hand them out before she leaves."

"The kids did pretty good tonight, didn't they?" Mark sounded a little surprised.

"Did you expect anything less? Myah's a good instructor."

"Oh, I knew that. But for most of these girls, this was their first public dancing gig, right? I don't know . . . I guess I was expecting something a bit more childish. And Katy . . . for all her grumbling and complaining, she actually did pretty good."

"I know, right?" She was so proud of her daughter, even though after this recital, Katy wanted to take a break. She wanted to try something different, and Tricia didn't have the heart to force her to continue something she wasn't enjoying. Unlike her cousin, Lyla, who was in swimming and dance and had been for a few years now, Katy, so far, had tried swimming, ballet, baseball, soccer, gymnastics, wall climbing, and dance. Maybe one day she'd find an activity she really liked.

"Has Aly called yet?"

Tricia shook her head. "They're probably all at the restaurant still. Give her another hour, and then she'll probably send a text asking about Lyla." Actually, she'd be surprised if it took her sister an hour. She knew tonight would be hard for her. If Scott was smart, he'd keep her occupied. She'd already talked with Rachel, who promised to keep her out as late as possible.

To say Alyson tended to be controlling was being generous. Aly was not just a control freak but a helicopter-style mother who wore the pants in her family and organized everyone and everything around her. She needed to be 100 percent in control of every facet of her life.

Tonight was the first time Aly had ever allowed her daughter to join a sleepover at someone else's home. It was a big deal. Tricia had been asking for more than a few years now to let Lyla stay over, but it never happened—until now. This recital-party sleepover came about not because she felt it important for the kids to celebrate like this but because she knew Lyla would be so excited that Alyson couldn't say no. Not to this. Not to a sleepover that included every single one of the girls from the class. Tricia had worked her magic on her sister, even to the point of letting Aly think this whole sleepover business was her idea.

"Doesn't it seem like Myah is taking a while?" Mark gave her a look, and she knew he thought she should check and see. First, she called the dogs and sent them into the back room where she'd arranged their dog beds for the night, and then closed the door. The last thing she needed was to have them underfoot when the pizza arrived.

When she went outside, Myah was sitting on the wicker chair on her front porch, a large box at her feet. She was hissing words into her phone.

Tricia debated whether to let her friend know she was there or just head back into the house.

"I'm beginning to hate you. You know that, right?" Myah said into the phone.

"Myah?" Tricia spoke her name softly, so as not to startle her. Myah waved her hand.

"Okay, Eddie, give me thirty minutes," Myah said before she hung up.

Tricia leaned against the wood railing and waited for Myah to regain her composure.

"I should have listened to you. Next time, make me listen to you," Myah muttered.

"You fell in love. You wouldn't listen to any of us," Tricia reminded her.

Myah and Eddie had been dance partners for years and got married just under two years ago. Tricia had never liked the man, felt he was an oily-tongued snake, but Myah wouldn't listen. She'd fallen under his spell, thinking she could help him change his ways.

"Next time, really make me listen." Myah picked up the box at her feet. "Help me hand these out? I need to meet with Eddie in half an hour."

Tricia held the door open for her. "Are you sure you want to do that tonight?"

"I need to." Myah said, her face downcast. "I just need to get it done, you know?"

"I know. Now, no frowns. Let's go give the girls these gift bags before the pizza arrives."

The basement buzzed with noise as they walked down the stairs, but it wasn't until Tricia opened the door that the full blast of having all these girls in one room hit her.

Myah whistled to grab their attention, and within moments, everyone had quieted down.

Tricia glanced around and noticed the girls had already rolled out their sleeping bags on the floor. Lyla was unobtrusively moving her sleeping bag closer to the wall.

Tricia couldn't help but smile. Like mother, like daughter.

While Myah talked to the girls about the amazing job they'd all done that night, the doorbell rang and Tricia made her way back upstairs. As Mark paid the delivery driver, Tricia set out the boxes of pizza along with plastic plates and napkins and let the boys get their slices first.

"How's the game going?" she asked David, her oldest.

"Good. Brandon and I are winning."

"Are you being nice to your brothers? Making sure they're having a good time too?" She'd taken him aside earlier and asked him to help keep things running smoothly among all the boys.

"Yes, Mom."

"And you remember what we said earlier, right? About leaving the girls alone?"

"You going to tell them the same thing?" He eyed her with interest.

"Of course." She caught the look he gave his friend Brandon. "Why?" she asked. "Is there something I should know?"

Her son shook his head. "I'll keep an eye on it. One of the girls has a crush on Brandon."

"Really?" Weren't the kids too young for this? So far Katy hadn't shown any indication of liking boys—either that or she was just blind to it. In all honestly, she wasn't ready for this stage. She was hoping to wait until Katy was at least fifteen or sixteen before she had to deal with broken hearts.

"Hey, Tricia?" Myah climbed the stairs. "The girls can smell the pizza. Are you ready for them?"

"Elijah, are you sure you don't want to take an extra slice?" Tricia reached for a slice of Hawaiian, her middle son's favorite, and placed it on his plate. "Send them up."

For the next ten minutes, the mayhem in her kitchen knew no bounds. The girls clustered together, whether sitting at the table, snagging stools from the counter, or standing beside their friends. The boys had migrated to the living room, and a few of the girls followed and sat on the floor, hoping to play the video game as well.

"I gotta run. You going to be okay?" Myah tapped Tricia on the shoulder, her bag slung over her shoulder.

Tricia laughed. "Are you seriously asking me that? I'll be fine. Go. Call me if you need me, okay?" She gave Myah a quick hug then watched her friend say good-bye to her daughter.

She didn't understand why Myah would meet Eddie so late at night but trusted she knew what she was doing.

It took another hour of corralling to get the kids into their respective areas and to explain the rules. Boys had to stay upstairs and girls in the basement—no sneaking around except to go to the bathroom.

"Seriously, Mom?" Katy had said. "As if we want the boys to bug us anyways." She stuck her tongue out toward her brothers before she turned and led the girls down to the basement.

"Should you follow?" Mark asked her once the kitchen was finally empty.

Tricia shook her head. "I'll give them a bit to get settled and figure out a game plan. That'll give us time to clean the kitchen at least."

Mark grabbed a garbage bag and began to throw away empty plates and cups, while Tricia stacked the empty pizza boxes.

"But I think tonight will be fine. They're only kids."

Mark laughed, dropped the bag, and grabbed her by the waist. "Only kids? Do you have any idea what I did between the ages of eleven and fourteen? I had found all my father's *Playboy* magazines and—"

"Disgusting." Tricia stopped him going any further. She was well aware of his escapades. They'd known each other since middle school.

"I'm just saying that maybe we shouldn't do any more coed sleepovers."

"Perhaps. If you're so worried about it, feel free to sleep with the boys tonight." She winked. "I'm sure they'd love to have an old man stink up the room with them."

"Who are you calling old?" He growled at her before lifting her up in his arms. "Could an old man do this?" He walked with her in his arms, then held her against the wall and kissed her.

"Stop." She laughed, pushing him away until her feet touched the ground again. "Behave yourself. The last thing we need is one of the kids seeing us make out in the kitchen and telling their parents."

"I'm surprised your mother never showed up. I would have thought she'd be in the thick of things tonight."

"She's coming in the morning to help me with breakfast." She would make pancakes to her heart's content and then help clean once all the kids left. Her mother was like Aly, a neat freak, so it was a win-win situation for Tricia, since it meant she'd have more help in the morning and a clean house in the end.

"Should we check in on the kids again before we head to bed?"

"Are you suggesting we embarrass our kids while we're saying good night?" Tricia could see the twinkle in her husband's gaze and chuckled. "I'll check in on the girls and see you upstairs."

When she opened the door downstairs, she was surprised to find a quiet room. The girls had a movie on, and everyone seemed to be watching it. She made her way across the room to where Katy and Keera sat on the sofa.

"Having fun?" she said quietly to her daughter.

"It's okay. Just watching a movie, and then we'll go to bed." Katy whispered back.

"Uh-huh. Just keep it down, okay? And no sneaking upstairs to the boys. Got it?" She gave Keera a look too.

"*As if.* Good night, Mom." Katy nudged her mom off the couch and leaned her head close to Keera, whispering something to her.

Tricia wove her way toward Lyla's sleeping bag, where the little girl was lying on her belly watching the movie. Tricia hunched down and gave her niece a kiss on the top of her head.

"Doing okay?" She asked.

Lyla nodded.

"If you need me, you know where I am."

"I'll be okay, Aunt Tricia, but thank you. Is Grandma coming over tomorrow for breakfast?"

Tricia smiled. She'd seen Ida hug Lyla hard earlier in the evening, and she must have told her.

"You bet she is. She's going to make her awesome pancakes just for us. Maybe you can help her?" Tricia figured if she gave Lyla something to look forward to in the morning, she might actually stay the whole night. Although, she didn't think that would be a problem, not from the way Lyla was acting.

"Good night." Lyla whispered, obviously wanting to watch the movie.

"Night, love."

This was working. It was actually working. She knew it would, had known from the moment she thought of it, but to actually have it working . . . She was good, if she did say so herself. Lyla's first full sleepover was going to be a success, and from here on out, Alyson couldn't say no to any future sleepovers. At least, she hoped she wouldn't.

She looked in on the boys, saying good night, and then headed upstairs to her bedroom. She kept the door open—that way they could hear if anyone was up and about.

"Think they'll all go to sleep like good little boys and girls?" Mark asked once they were settled in bed.

"Are you kidding me? I got the little angel act from the girls. How were the boys?"

He shrugged. "About the same. They swore they were going to watch one movie and then go to sleep."

"Right." They both said at the same time.

"I found our old baby monitor in the closet and set it up in the kitchen where the kids can't see it." He leaned over and picked up the monitor from the floor. "Still works, see?" He turned it on and dialed the volume up loud enough so they could hear in the background the movie the boys were watching. He turned it down to a low murmur and set it on his nightstand.

"Good move." She was very impressed. "Now, if you can keep from snoring, we might actually hear it if they try something."

"When," Mark corrected her. "'Cause you know it's a *when* and not an *if*."

Tricia sighed. "How late should we stay up then?"

"Why don't we watch our own movie and turn the volume up a bit. If they know we're still awake, it might make them think twice." Mark reached for the remote and turned on the television in their bedroom. "Although, from the looks I caught between Keera and Brandon . . ." He let his voice trail off.

"Keera? No way. One of the other girls, maybe. But not our Keera."

"If you say so." Mark turned off his bedside light and scrolled through the channels to find a movie.

By the time their movie was over, everything in the house was quiet, so Tricia relaxed and attempted to fall asleep. Then she heard the creak of a door closing.

"Did you hear that?" Mark asked, somewhat sleepily.

"I did." She groaned, not really wanting to get up. "It's either the bathroom door or one of the boys' rooms."

"Think one of the boys wanted to sleep in their own bed?"

Tricia rolled over to look at Mark. "If it's one of the boys, you should check it out."

Mark yawned, and pulled himself out of bed, arching his back as he did. "Don't they realize it's almost three in the morning?" He shuffled his way out of the bedroom and down the hall, opening up doors and closing them until Tricia heard him call for her.

CHAPTER THREE

MYAH
LATE FRIDAY NIGHT

The smugness of her soon-to-be ex-husband irritated Myah to the point that she wanted to throw his beer in his face and walk away. But she couldn't. There were too many people around who knew her, and she refused to make a fuss in public.

Maybe one day she would. The next time she walked up to him making out with some trashy bimbo, she would for sure.

"I'm done, Eddie." Myah said between clenched teeth. "Why is this woman here?"

"It's okay to admit you're a little bit jealous."

That was it. There was no next time. She reached across to grab his beer, but he swiped it before she could.

"Come now, Myah, love. Don't be like that." He tipped his glass to his lips and drank until the beer was gone. "Let's not make this difficult. I thought we'd agreed that from the beginning."

Exasperated beyond belief, Myah sat back in her chair. Not make it difficult? Did he just say that? After what she'd walked in to see?

"If *you* want to make a fool of yourself in front of people we know, go for it. But please, don't embarrass me."

"If I'd known you were going to be early, I wouldn't have. We just got . . . carried away." Eddie gave a slight shrug of his shoulders. "You know how it is."

Myah rolled her eyes. Yes, she knew how it was. Eddie was a man who lived by his passions, and she really shouldn't be too surprised. But she was still upset.

"Eddie, I'm tired. It's been a long night, and I'm not up for playing games." When he lifted his empty glass to the waitress, Myah sighed. "Don't you think you've had enough?"

"Why? I thought we were celebrating. You had a lovely little recital at our theater, where our little girl was the star of the show. I think that deserves another round, doesn't it?"

"All the kids did well," she reminded him, even though secretly she agreed.

"Oh come on, love. You know she was the best. She has us as teachers, after all."

Myah drummed her fingers on the table. It wasn't even worth it.

"Eddie, we need to talk. Seriously." A waitress came over, dropped off another draft beer for Eddie, and brought her a warm tea. Eddie, of course, gave the waitress a wink, while Myah just said a quiet thank-you.

"Then talk. That's why I'm here. You know I'll always drop everything for you, babe."

Ugh. Why had it taken her so long to see him for the man he was?

She reached into her purse and pulled out a long brown envelope. "I'm ready." She dropped the envelope on the table and pushed it toward him. "Our marriage is over, and we both know it."

Eddie stared at the envelope but didn't touch it.

"Are you sure, love? I'm not ready to lose you."

Myah laughed. She actually laughed. Who was he kidding? Certainly not her.

"Oh come on now, Eddie. Think of the publicity you can gain from this. Who knows? Perhaps you can make a comeback. That's why you put so much energy and money into redoing the theater, isn't it?" Call her cynical, but she'd never known her husband, soon-to-be ex-husband, to do anything if it didn't benefit him in some way.

Even their marriage had been for more than just love. She knew that now. She realized it only a few short months after those butter-fly feelings had flown away and reality came crashing down, when they stepped away from the hectic tour schedule to raise Keera with normalcy.

"I don't need the spotlight again, Myah. I need you. I need Keera. I need my family in my life. Please don't do this." For a moment, Eddie looked like he was going to cry.

"Oh please. You like the idea of family more than the reality of it."

He reached out to grab her hand. "No, I'm serious, Myah. Since I moved out, I've been lonely. I've realized how empty my life is. Sleeping at the theater hall isn't home. Home is with you and our daughter."

She pulled her hand away and crossed her arms. Where was this talk of family when she needed it the most? Why now when it meant nothing? Until she'd asked him to move out, he'd never shown any interest in being much of a father to Keera. Not unless it involved dancing.

"She's not your daughter, Eddie. I asked you to officially adopt her, and you refused. Or do you not remember that?" That act alone had been the first indication that she'd picked the wrong man. It was too bad she hadn't asked him to do this before their marriage.

"My biggest regret. That and cheating on you. I wish I could turn back time." He bowed his head for a moment before looking up and giving her a soft smile. "Give me a second chance, please."

"You were kissing another woman ten minutes ago!"

"Ah, Myah, you break my heart." He clutched at his chest as if his heart were actually breaking.

"Just sign the papers, please."

"What about Keera? Doesn't she need a father?"

Taken back, Myah wasn't sure how to respond. What was going on with him? A midlife crisis? Was he realizing his youth was behind him? Did he see a spark in Keera, one that he now wanted to be a part of nurturing?

"I don't know, Eddie. You tell me, what about my daughter?"

If he thought to placate her with a softening of his eyes and his charming smile, he was sadly mistaken. And, if he thought to use her daughter for his gain, he was in for a rude awakening.

"Whoa. I know that look. Calm down, sweetheart. I just don't want to be out of her life. That's it. I promise." He held his hands up in mock surrender.

"You're not in her life now, Eddie."

"That's not true."

"Just sign the papers. Please. Everything is amicable and very detailed." She just wanted this over.

"What about the theater?"

She gave him a look of exasperation. "What about it? We've already discussed all of this—we have equal ownership. It's profitable and the only venue in town for shows. We'll keep it the way it is, other than you now occupy the upstairs apartment and owe rent. We already agreed on all of this." The theater was the least of her worries, if she was honest. At least with that, she knew she had a steady income stream.

"I just wanted to make sure none of that changes." His fingers touched the envelope, and she held her breath, waiting to see if he'd open it. "So you want me to sign these papers, and then what?"

She rolled her eyes. "Are you for real? We're getting a divorce, Eddie. There is no *and then what* for us. All that will remain is the theater. We'll be business associates, sharing a venue where we both teach classes and hold events. We will live our own separate lives. Is that what you want to hear?"

He let go of the envelope, and at that moment, she knew this was just one more game for him. She'd had enough. She gathered her purse and started to stand when he reached out and gripped her arm, stopping her.

"No. That's not what I want to hear. You've never answered me about Keera. About our daughter. I want to remain in her life."

The slow boil that flowed through her blood increased in temperature, and if she wasn't careful, she was about to create a scene.

She stood up from her seat and planted her palms on the table and glared.

"She is not *our* daughter. She is mine. Do you understand that Eddie? Mine. As for her seeing you—that will be up to her. Although, I have a funny feeling, since you've never shown any interest in her apart from her dancing, that she isn't going to care either way."

"Don't be so sure about that."

Maybe it was his tone, but a little bit of apprehension wormed its way into her heart. *Don't be so sure about that.* What did he mean?

"I asked Keera if we could do breakfast tomorrow, to celebrate, since I obviously didn't see her tonight. I want her to know how awesome she did, how proud I am of her," he explained, his tone very different from just moments ago.

"She didn't tell me that. When did you ask her?" Why didn't Keera mention this?

He leaned back in his seat with a self-satisfied look he couldn't hide even if he wanted to. "Last night."

Myah stood up straight and looked down on the man she once loved. "Don't you think I'm the one you should be asking? Not Keera. Eddie, she's not your daughter. You have no legal right to her." Why did she have to keep reminding him of this?

His smugness disappeared when he realized she was serious.

"I'm sorry, love." He stood up beside her and grabbed her hands, holding them tight in his own. "You're right. I have to respect the line. Of course I'll sign the papers, if that is what you want. But please, please don't take Keera from my life. I know I'm not perfect, but . . . she needs a father figure, something you've said yourself. Let me be that. Please? I won't ask for much. Maybe I can take her out for breakfasts or lunches, keep teaching her routines, and . . ." He suddenly stopped, and Myah knew instantly why.

"Ah, yes, those moves you've been teaching her behind my back. You didn't think I'd noticed? You know how I feel about her learning the more advanced routines. She's not going to be competing, so she doesn't need to know those intricate moves."

He hung his head as if in shame. "I'm sorry, Myah. That's my fault. She . . . she said she was interested and wanted to see if she could do it, so I offered to teach her a little here and there to see if it was something she truly wanted."

"Without asking me first? Eddie . . ." Her exasperation with him just hit the limit. "It's not okay for Keera to keep secrets from me, Eddie. Not okay." She clutched her purse tightly in her hands. "Those moves, those secret dance lessons, they stop. Now." She waited for acknowledgment in his gaze and stared at him until she received it. "You want to build a relationship with Keera so she can have a good fatherly influence in her life? Then it starts with not keeping secrets from me. Got it?"

She didn't know why she was giving in, why she was agreeing to this, and yet, here she was. "I hate you. You do realize that, right?"

He had the audacity to smile at her right then. "I know, love. You've always been one for fierce passions. I'll take your love or hatred any day, as long as it never turns to indifference." He leaned forward as if to kiss her on the lips, but she turned and walked away from him.

"What about tomorrow?" He called out after her.

She ignored him. She needed to talk to her daughter first before she made any decisions about breakfast.

CHAPTER FOUR

IDA
SATURDAY MORNING

Ida's mind wandered as she washed the dishes in the sink. Scrub, dip, rinse, and repeat. She once hated the process, forced to clean the plates and cutlery of her family of ten growing up. As a young child, everyone in the home had a chore. Her brothers took care of the outside work with their father, keeping the yard tidy, fixing their car and the farm equipment, and cleaning out the stalls. Two of her older sisters fed the animals daily, while the other girls took care of housework. Her mother had been a hard taskmaster. With twelve people in the house, including two cats and three dogs, one would expect a farmhouse to be dirty, cluttered, and utterly chaotic.

But Frau Becker did not believe in messiness and instilled that same belief in her children. Ida's chores were dishes and keeping the kitchen counter clean.

The day she'd convinced Gordon to install a dishwasher had been one of the best days of her life. So why was she doing dishes now, when Tricia had a dishwasher as well?

Because it helped to clear her mind.

"I thought you hated doing dishes?" Her husband, Gordon, said as he came up behind her.

"Ja, ich weiß." I know. She glanced over her shoulder. "But the dishwasher is already full. I thought I told her to use paper plates."

"I did, Mother." Tricia held up a large black garbage bag as she stuffed napkins into it. "We ran out, though, for breakfast. A certain someone didn't pick up enough paper plates last night." Tricia pointed to her husband.

"I did offer to wash the dishes," Mark said.

"Enough, you two. I don't mind, and I'm happy to help." Ida shook her head at her daughter and son-in-law. There was a tension in the air that came from the two of them, despite their efforts to hide it. A mother could tell these things.

"Who's left?" Mark asked Tricia as loud thumping music came from the top of the stairs.

"Just Lyla and Keera," Tricia said.

"And they listen to that loud music?" Ida was a bit shocked. She knew the girls were into music now, always with headphones attached to their ears, but the music seemed especially loud.

"I think it's one of the songs from their routine." Tricia rubbed her face and dropped the garbage bag. "I'll go deal with it."

"No." Mark laid his hand on her arm. "I've got it."

Ida waited until Mark was upstairs. "What's going on between you two?" She was finished with the dishes and wiped her wet hands on her apron.

"Nothing. Why?" Tricia hedged. She began to rub her left wrist, moving her cuffed bracelet out of the way. She stopped, pushing the cuff back down into place, when she realized Ida was watching her.

"Because you two seem grumpy, that's why," Gordon said to his daughter. Ida was surprised he'd noticed the tension too.

"We're just tired. Having that many kids probably wasn't my greatest idea." Tricia then yawned.

"They were up all night, were they? Any fooling around?" Ida asked.

Gordon sat down at the now clean kitchen table. "I told you," he said to Ida.

"Told her what?" Tricia turned to face her father. "What did you say? What did he say?"

Ida went and poured herself a fresh cup of coffee. "He's just trying to get under your skin. Ignore him."

"I told your mother something was going to happen last night. Kids will be kids. I remember what you and your sister were like at that age. No doubt they were all sneaking off with one another. It's those hormones." Gordon teased his daughter, completely oblivious to the way she was clutching her hands. Couldn't he see she wasn't in the mood to be teased? And that this was a subject he knew nothing about?

"Still, du Narr!" Quiet, you fool! If he would only just leave things alone.

"Grandma, no German!" Gord Jr., Tricia's youngest and named after her father, walked into the kitchen and gave his mother a hug, wrapping his arms around her waist. "What did she say?" he asked.

"She just called your grandpa an old fool and told him to be quiet."

Ida caught the glare her daughter gave her father. He deserved it too.

"What would you know about kids? And your daughters were never like that." Ida tsk-tsked then went to sit down beside him at the table.

"I remember enough. Especially what it's like to be a boy in a house full of girls." Gordon winked at his grandson, and Ida placed her hand on her husband's arm, warning him to stop.

"Brandon and a few of the girls were found in David's bedroom last night." Gord Jr. piped up.

"Tricia, no!" This was news. Why hadn't Tricia told her this before now?

"Why don't you go join your brothers now?" Tricia gave her son a frown before shooing him back where he came from. "It wasn't that big of a deal," she said, once her son had left.

"Not that big of a deal? Of course it is." Ida said.

"It's not. And it's being dealt with, and besides"—she looked up at Mark who was coming back down the stairs—"nothing happened."

Ida tightened her lips but didn't say anything. Nothing happened, her foot. How was she dealing with it? What girls?

"I just saw Myah pull up. Keera's getting her stuff together now," Mark said quietly to Tricia.

So Keera was involved. That poor child. Growing up fatherless, and then having Eddie, a womanizer, be part of her life. No wonder that girl was sneaking around at night with boys. The kids these days, they get too much leeway, with too much freedom. Not like when she was a child.

"I'll go meet her," Tricia said.

When Tricia left the room, Ida decided to find out from her son-in-law what was going on.

"Nothing too serious, Ida. Just kids being kids," Mark said. "I did worse at their age. Trust me. Tricia is just upset because it was Keera and Katy."

Ida gasped.

"Calm down, woman," Gordon shook his head at her. "Sounds like it's all been handled, and there's no reason for you to cause a scene."

"A scene? Who said I was causing a scene? And don't you tell me to calm down, old man. I have a right to be concerned." Ida glared at her husband.

"He's right," Mark interjected. "It's been handled. Gordon, I need to run over to the Peterson's job site to take a look at some issues. Want to join me?"

Gordon shook his head. "No, I trust you to handle it. These old bones can't climb all those stairs at their place. Why someone would want a three story plus basement is beyond me."

Ida frowned. "If I need to go home, I'm sure Tricia can take me. Go. Get out of my hair." Gordon had retired from the day-to-day work at Wilhem & Sons, but he couldn't stay home all the time. He needed to stay busy. Otherwise he became a grumpy old bear, which in turn made her miserable. The golden life of retirement quickly lost its appeal with the husband underfoot.

Ida and Gordon sat at the table in silence, when Tricia walked back in and called up to Keera to tell her that her mom had arrived.

"I'm going to go have coffee with Myah for a bit. Do you mind?" Tricia asked her. "I shouldn't be gone longer than an hour."

Ida shook her head. "Go. Enjoy the coffee. The kids and I will make cookies while you're gone."

"Thanks, Mom. I should be back before Aly comes to pick up Lyla. There's a dance practice today, just to go over last night, so I won't be long."

"Katy's not going though, right?"

Tricia nodded. "Right. She's done, for now. We'll see how long that lasts though. I thought she was really enjoying something for once."

The girls all came down the stairs, a bit somber.

"I hear you girls are going to make cookies with Grandma. Have fun." Tricia gave Katy a kiss on the top of her head and then hugged Lyla. "Thanks for coming over last night, sweetie. I'm glad you had a fun time."

Ida caught the glances between the girls and knew something was up. Maybe it was nothing. Maybe it was just whispered secrets that had nothing to do with anything other than being a girl at a sleepover.

"Thanks, Mom, for staying." She took a step toward Ida. "Please, let me handle things, okay?" She said quietly.

Ida sighed. "Whatever." She threw up her hands and then followed the crowd out to the front door.

"I hear you're having breakfast with Eddie," Tricia said as Keera put on her shoes and coat. "That must be why you didn't eat a lot of pancakes this morning."

"Just not hungry." Keera grabbed her bag and headed out the door.

"Okay then," Tricia mumbled before she followed her. She waved good-bye to Katy and Lyla, smiled at her mom, and closed the door.

"All right," Ida clapped her hands together. "Who's in the mood to make cookies?" She led the girls back into the kitchen muttering beneath her breath.

"What's the matter with you now?" Gordon poured himself a coffee.

"Etwas ist los, und ich bin nicht glücklich." Something is going on, and I'm not happy. Her husband gave her a look telling her to be quiet with the kids around.

"Grandma!" Gord Jr. popped up from the other side of the counter and wiggled his finger at her. "No German. We can't understand what you're saying." He admonished her.

"I know, I know." She shook her head in disgust. Why Tricia didn't teach her children to speak the mother tongue, she'd never understand. *"Vielleicht sollten Sie dann etwas Deutsche lernen."*

"Grandma." This time it was Elijah who huffed at her from the kitchen table. "What did you say?"

"That maybe you should learn a little German then, no?" She used to speak to her grandchildren in German until Alyson asked her to stop. She'd assumed Tricia felt the same way.

"How?" Elijah seemed interested, which made Ida happy.

"We could teach you." Gordon stood there, his arms crossed over his massive puffed out chest.

"I used to sing lullabies to you as babies. Do you remember?" Ida smiled, the memory warming her heart. Gordon had built a rocking chair for the baby room, and she'd sit there, rocking the little ones to sleep to give Tricia a breather, and she'd sing the songs her own Mutter would sing.

"What would you sing?" Elijah left his seat and came to stand by the counter.

Gordon winked at her before he placed his arm around his grandson's shoulder. "You don't want to remember. Trust me. Your Oma has the voice of a dying cat."

Elijah's eyes grew round, while Ida tried not to laugh. "Your Opa doesn't sound any better."

"Can I"—Elijah lowered his voice—"can I call you Oma and Opa instead of Grandma and Grandpa?"

Tears pricked at Ida's eyes at her grandson's question. "You used to call us that, you know?" She wasn't sure when it stopped, probably around the same time they stopped speaking in German to them.

"Us too?"

Ida turned toward her girls, who stood there with their arms around each other. She went over and gave them both a hug. "Of course." She said.

Katy struggled to get out of her embrace. "Can we make cookies now? Please?"

"Pretty please?" Lyla snuggled in closer to Ida and sighed with happiness.

Ida couldn't get over how different the girls were. As cousins, they'd been inseparable from the time they were born, and now as young girls, they continued to be the best of friends, even if so very different in nature. Lyla was prim and proper, the perfect little girl, whereas Katy could be a little hellion masquerading as an angel when she wanted to be.

"How do you say cookies in German, Oma?" Elijah asked.

"*Kekse*. And your Oma here makes the best ones I've ever tasted. Even better than my own Mutter." Gordon smiled.

"And that means 'mother,' right?"

"*Ja.*"

"Why are you speaking in German?" Katy's face was scrunched up, and Ida shook her head.

"Monster cookies, Lyla?" She dropped a kiss onto her granddaughter's head.

"Can we? Please?"

"Katherine, let's get all the ingredients out, shall we?" Ida clapped her hands and then went to grab an apron out of the drawer. Things could get messy, but messy was okay when it was created with love.

"While the women work, how about we challenge your brothers to a new game on that fancy machine you have." Gordon steered Elijah out of the kitchen and back into the living room. "The winner gets extra cookies fresh from the oven."

Ida turned her attention back to the kitchen where the girls were gathering supplies out of the pantry.

"Sounds like we're going to need to make a lot," Lyla said as she grabbed a large mixing bowl and wooden spoons.

"Should we make extra for you to take home?"

At her question, Lyla shook her head. "Mom won't let me eat them if I do."

"What about your dad then?"

Lyla nodded. "He'll let me eat them." A wide smile grew on her face. "Let's just not tell Mom, okay?"

She was a bit surprised at Lyla's duplicity. Not tell her mom? Since when had Lyla ever gone against Alyson?

"Or we can just make sure we eat them all before your mom comes and picks you up. That way you're not lying or anything," Katy said. She paused in opening the lids on the sugar and flour containers.

Lyla's lips thinned, but she didn't say a word.

The silence between the two girls was palpable as Ida had them follow the recipe she'd been taught as a young child. Katy had wanted to use the mixer, but Ida wouldn't allow it. The best cookies were the ones made completely from scratch—and that included having to hand mix them.

"Shall I tell you a story of the first time I remember making cookies with my own Oma?"

The girls perked up at this, smiles gracing their faces. They always loved her stories, whether it was from when she was a child on a farm in Germany or stories of their moms when they were young girls.

"Did you make monster cookies too?" Lyla asked.

Ida shook her head. "The cookies I made are called *Engelsaugen*. Do you know what that means?"

Both girls shook their heads.

"'Angel eyes.' They were my father's favorite cookie ever, and out of all my sisters, I made them the best."

"Do you still make them?" Katy asked.

Ida pretended to be shocked. "Still make them? Of course I do. You eat them every Christmas, my dear little girl."

"Can you teach me how to make them this year, Oma?"

Ida stilled. The last time Lyla had called her Oma had been . . . years ago.

She gave Lyla a hug. "Of course I will, darling girl. We'll make the best *Engelsaugen* cookies ever." Anything to place a smile on this girl's face and to make her laugh.

CHAPTER FIVE

ALYSON

"Good morning, beautiful," Scott whispered in Alyson's ear. "Breakfast smells amazing." He nuzzled her neck, while she swatted him away.

"If you don't want your breakfast burned, then you should let me finish." She quickly kissed his cheek before checking on the omelet she was making.

She was excited to pick up Lyla this morning and hear all about the sleepover, but she wanted to enjoy the morning with Scott before he left for work. It had been a long time since it had just been the two of them, and she wanted to savor each moment.

"Last night was fun. We should do it more often." Scott poured himself a coffee and leaned against the counter.

"It was. Everyone we talked to seemed to enjoy themselves, which was great."

"Do you think Lyla had fun?" Scott asked. There was a look in his eye, a twinkling, as if he knew she was trying hard not to bring their daughter up.

"I hope so." She flipped the omelet onto a plate, cutting it in half and transferring part of it onto a smaller plate. She added turkey bacon to the plates, and then handed Scott his.

"Seriously? No real bacon?" He pouted for a moment before taking a slice and biting into it. "It doesn't even taste like bacon," he muttered, taking his plate and coffee over to the breakfast bar.

"Thanks for breakfast, Aly. You're welcome, Scott," Alyson said quietly.

"Thank you for breakfast, my dear sweet wife." Scott got the hint.

"You're welcome, my dear handsome husband." She teased him before sitting beside him.

"What do you think about maybe going away one weekend? Just the two of us?" Scott asked.

"Where?"

He shrugged. "Paul was telling me about that bed-and-breakfast place he's taking Rachel. I thought we could do something similar."

Alyson ate her omelet and didn't say anything right away. She felt torn. Yes, it would be nice to get away. It was something they used to do all the time before Lyla was born . . . but it meant leaving Lyla, and she wasn't sure about that.

"She never called, so I assume that's a good thing, right?" It was as if Scott knew what she was thinking.

"I hope so, but she's still a bit young . . ."

"Just think about it, okay? I miss us . . . when we can just be a couple, not parents or anything else. Don't you miss it too?"

She took a sip of her coffee and frowned. "But we are parents, Scott. It's not like we can just ignore that part of our lives whenever we feel like it. We both knew our lives would change once we had Lyla."

"You know what I mean," Scott said. He ate the remainder of his breakfast in silence.

What was she supposed to do? Say yes, that she'd love to go away without knowing more information? When? Where? For how long—one night or two? What about his work and Lyla's dance and swim schedule? Of course, she would love to go away, but it wasn't always possible. Was it fair of him to sulk just because she didn't give a resounding yes?

"How long do you think you'll be today?" she asked after he'd pushed his plate away. She got up and filled his thermos with coffee and then another with water.

"I hope to be home midafternoon. I'll get the framing finished today, so we can send a crew in to mud and tape on Monday." He grabbed the thermoses and hooked them onto one of his workbags. "What's the plan for today with Lyla?"

Alyson began to clean things up. "She's making cookies with mom this morning, and then I'll pick her up for dance."

"There's dance today? After her recital yesterday?" He stopped. "Why not give the kids a day off?"

"It won't be a full practice, just something fun to reward the kids for yesterday and stuff." She'd questioned the same thing, especially after the kids had had a late night with the sleepover, but Myah convinced her that it would be a good outlet for the tired kids.

She hoped she was right.

"Well, if she's not too tired tonight, why don't we all go out? Dinner and a movie or maybe a movie and dessert after?"

"So another late night? Do you plan on being home all day tomorrow to deal with her grumpiness?" Scott was all about the fun, but unfortunately, she was the one who had to deal with the consequences.

"I'll leave it up to you, then. You know best, I suppose." There was something in his tone that put her on edge.

"What's the issue?" She asked.

He just shrugged and grabbed his bags. "Nothing. I'll see you tonight."

He left, while she stood there trying to figure out what set him off. She hated when he walked away from her like that. If he had a problem with her, he should tell her, talk it out, deal with it. Face it head on and get it out of the way now rather than let it fester, which is what he was going to do.

She poured herself another cup of coffee. So where did that leave her? She didn't want a late night for Lyla. She was probably already going to be little miss grumpy pants.

She reached for her phone and typed a message to Scott.

Let's order in, Lyla's choice, and watch a movie at home. You can run out and get ice cream after dinner maybe? Or make our own sundaes?

It meant more sugar, which really wouldn't help matters, but it would still be a fun night, right? Give and take—isn't that what marriage and parenting were all about?

See, she could relax, stop being so stringent, and have fun.

She called her sister's house, to prove to herself she could be fun.

"Hi, Mom." Lyla answered. Her voice was chipper and happy, and any misgivings Alyson had had about her daughter's first sleepover disappeared.

"Hey, honey. How's it going so far? Did you have a good time last night?"

"Oma is baking cookies with us. Chocolate chip. And she said I can bring some home—is that okay? I thought Daddy might like some."

Alyson couldn't help but be surprised by the term *Oma*. Lyla never called her grandmother anything but *Grandma*.

"I'm sure your dad would like some. Make sure to make enough, and we can do ice cream sandwiches for dessert tonight." See . . . fun. She could do it.

"Really?" The surprise in her daughter's voice irked her. Well, okay, maybe it was warranted, since she rarely allowed her daughter to have sugar.

Maybe instead of ice cream they could do frozen yogurt. If she started it now, she could make up a homemade batch, which would be a lot healthier than the store-bought kind.

"Really. Have fun making cookies with Grandma, and I'll see you in an hour, okay?" That would give her enough time to make the creamy mixture, clean up, and get over there before dance practice.

Within the hour, Alyson had made a batch of vanilla frozen yogurt that was now setting up in the freezer. She'd cleaned her kitchen from breakfast and did a load of laundry. After dance practice, she could relax a little with Lyla and find out how last night went without distraction.

When she arrived at Tricia's, she rang the doorbell before walking in and followed the delicious aroma of freshly baked cookies. Ida was in her glory with her grandchildren surrounding her. Her apron was dirty, the kitchen a disaster, but she was smiling and talking to the kids . . . in German?

Lyla sat at the kitchen table and was adding cookies to a storage container. "Hi, Mom. How many cookies do you think we'll need for tonight? Oma let me make the first batch, since I have to leave first."

"*Oma* did, did she?" Alyson stressed the German word for grandmother and raised an eyebrow at her mother.

Ida just shrugged. "*Es ist Zeit, sie die Muttersprache zu lernen.*"

"They already know their mother language—it's English." Lyla had never expressed any interest in learning German, and if she were honest, Alyson would prefer to keep it that way. She had no interest in her heritage. It had been shoved down her throat time and time again during her childhood, until Alyson had grown up hating being told to be a good German girl. What was wrong with just being a good girl?

"Where's Tricia?" Alyson expected her sister to be right in the mix of things.

When Ida didn't answer immediately, Alyson turned to her daughter, suddenly suspicious.

"She went out for coffee with Keera's mom." It was Katy who finally offered up the information.

Alyson sighed but kept all thoughts to herself. One look from her mother confirmed that Ida knew how she felt.

"Ready to go, Lyla?" They had at least forty-five minutes before class started, but she didn't really want to stick around. "Thanks for the cookies, Mom." She took the container full of cookies from her daughter, then grabbed her bags while Lyla put her shoes and coat on.

"Sure you need to run so soon? She has time before her class, doesn't she?" Ida followed them out into the hallway.

"How long has Tricia been gone?"

Ida shrugged, as if it didn't matter, as if she didn't care how Alyson felt about Lyla being here without Tricia present.

"See you on Sunday, Mom." Alyson readjusted her grip on the bag she carried and attempted to smile.

"So . . . how was it last night?" she asked Lyla once they were in the car and driving down the road.

"It was fine." Her daughter stared out the window. "Can we get some lunch before practice? Maybe a smoothie?"

It was *fine*? "That sounds good. We can stop at the little café across from the dance studio—you like their smoothies, right?"

Lyla nodded and continued to stare out the window.

Perhaps she was just tired. Lyla was an introvert, much like herself, and being with so many people for that long probably overwhelmed her. So Alyson gave her daughter some space. They sat in silence at the café while Lyla sipped at her strawberry-banana smoothie and Alyson drank a carrot juice and ate one of their specialty items—a house-made protein bar made with coconut oil.

Lyla seemed to perk up halfway through her smoothie, and she began to talk about the recital, asking questions about the routine and what Alyson's favorite part had been.

After buying a coffee to go, together they walked across the street to the dance studio at the back of the theater. Alyson was impressed with how Myah had managed to turn one of the larger rooms into a real studio. Alyson wondered what would happen with the theater if Myah and Eddie divorced. It would be sad to lose something that had become so integral to their community.

While Lyla went to change into her dance clothes, Alyson settled into the seat nearest the girls who had already arrived and were stretching on the mats. Alyson sipped her hot coffee and checked the time. Myah was late. Again. This was the fifth time since September, and from the looks of the other mothers around her, she wasn't the only one who noticed.

"Wonder what the excuse will be this time." Melinda Brown leaned over and stage-whispered into her ear. "If her husband wasn't so expensive, half the moms in here would have signed their girls up for his class. Hell, half the moms would have signed themselves up too."

Alyson pretended she didn't hear that last part. Sure, Eddie Mendez had looks to sweep any woman off her feet, but he also had the character of a slug.

When Alyson caught the nods of agreement from the other women around them, she reached for her phone and sent her sister a text.

Where's Myah? She's not at class.

"Someone should say something." Melinda nudged Alyson in the arm.

"Feel free," Alyson said quietly as she waited for her sister to respond.

No idea. She left here twenty minutes ago. She told Eddie she wanted a divorce and wasn't doing too good this morning, her sister replied.

So they were getting a divorce. That would be hard on Myah.

Think she'll show up? Maybe Myah mentioned something to Tricia.

"But you're friends with her." Melinda wouldn't let the subject go.

"I'm not the one with the issue though, Melinda. You are. Or someone else should say something if it bothers them so much. Honestly—I wouldn't stress over today. It's just a fun class—Myah already told us that." While she was a little bothered Myah hadn't shown up yet, she wasn't going to admit that, especially not to Melinda.

"Fun class or not, we deserve her full attention. I mean, the kids deserve it. God knows I wouldn't mind sleeping in a few mornings a week. I get why the kids have dance lessons in the morning on the weekends, but do we really need to come to yoga lessons during the week?" Melinda grumbled.

Melinda complained about the early morning practices every other week it seemed. But seriously, she didn't have to sign her daughter up for the new yoga classes Myah offered if she didn't like mornings. Alyson turned slightly in her chair and crossed her legs before giving Lyla a small wave. Lyla waved back, a timid smile on her face.

No idea. Tricia had finally responded.

Alyson put her phone away and watched her daughter interact with the other girls.

"Hey." Melinda nudged her in the arm again. "Maryanne is having a sleepover next weekend, and we were wondering if Lyla would want to come? It'll just be other girls from dance and a few from their classroom."

Another sleepover so soon?

"Who else will be there exactly?"

"Oh, you know, the usual girls." She began to name off most of the girls in the dance class. "And their friends from school, of course. Sarah, Alicia, Rose, and of course, Katy." Melinda smiled.

"Does Maryanne go to a lot of sleepovers?" Alyson asked.

Melinda nodded. "She loves them. She mentioned Lyla isn't at many, so I'm not sure if it's just her crazy schedule or if she's not into sleepovers, but I thought we'd give it a try at least. I hope she'll come—she'll have so much fun."

"Let me ask her." Since she really had no idea how last night went, she wasn't sure if Lyla would want to do more overnight parties. Her first reaction was to say no, but she knew Scott wouldn't be happy if she didn't at least mention it to Lyla first.

"Is she still in swimming? How is that going?" Melinda persisted in creating small talk, and despite her mind being on other issues, Alyson turned to her so she didn't come across as rude.

"It's good and she loves it. Is Maryanne interested in joining again?"

"It's too expensive. I don't know how you can afford that plus dance. Don't they realize we're not made out of money?"

Alyson nodded. It was expensive, but she and Scott had known that going in and decided it was worth it. "Are there other groups that don't cost as much, if it's something she wants to do?"

Melinda shook her head. "Honestly, I don't have the time for it. Besides, I don't think we should keep kids so active. Let them learn to do things on their own instead of always being in scheduled activities. Whatever happened to downtime?"

Alyson didn't agree at all. "I think if the kids want to do it and we can make it happen for them, then it's better that than playing on their electronics all day, staring at a screen."

"There must be a perfect medium in there somewhere, right?" Melinda smiled and then nodded toward the doors, where someone Alyson didn't recognize stepped in.

"I'm so sorry for being late. Myah had to cancel last minute. I hear you all had a fabulous recital last night, so today we're just going to have fun and work on those new yoga stretches Myah showed you all last week. How does that sound?" The girls all clapped. "Have you all been warming up? I'm Jessie. Just let me just get the music going, and we can get started." Jessie kept up a running commentary as she dropped her bag on the floor. The girl was young, probably fresh out of school, and thanks to Myah's cancelation, the girls were probably going to have a free-for-all lesson.

"Great," Melinda muttered. "Should have just stayed home."

Alyson rolled her eyes. "You do realize the Saturday classes are optional, right?" Unable to take anymore, she pulled out her phone, ignored the woman beside her, and spent the next half hour scrolling through recipe websites to find suggestions for dinner. She almost jumped when Lyla appeared at her side.

"Ready?"

Alyson placed her phone back in her purse. "Ready." She couldn't wait to leave. She'd had enough listening to Melinda and a few of the other mothers grumble and complain all throughout the class about Myah's absence.

"So tell me," Alyson said to her daughter as they stood at the counter, mixing ingredients for muffins. "How was it last night?"

Lyla shrugged as she poured agave nectar into a measuring spoon. "It was fun. I'm really tired though."

"What time did you get to sleep last night?"

Again with another shrug. "We watched a movie and then some videos and played some games. It was late though. I fell asleep a few times and then woke up from the laughing."

"Sounds like a regular sleepover." It felt like pulling teeth to get Lyla to talk about it, and that wasn't like her at all. "What movie did you watch?"

The look her daughter gave her was priceless.

"What? I'm curious. I wish I had been there, and I want to know all about it. Did everyone get along? Everyone behaved, right?"

She thought for sure Lyla would say yes and was surprised when her daughter hesitated before answering.

"Well . . . Katy and Keera snuck out of the basement for a bit." She looked at Alyson from the corner of her eye before looking away.

Katy and Keera? "They did? Where did they go?"

Lyla shrugged. Again. She was really beginning to hate these noncommittal gestures from her daughter.

"Lyla . . ."

"I don't know. I thought they just went upstairs to grab some food and bring it back down. Katy said she had some chocolate chips hidden in her room."

The batter was ready, so Alyson began to spoon it into the waiting muffin tray.

"You don't do that, do you?" She attempted to remain casual, but inside, she couldn't help feeling a little worried.

She glanced over at her daughter, who stared at her with eyes wide open.

"I don't. I never have. Daddy said that's how ants get in your room."

"He did, did he?" That probably gave her nightmares. What was he thinking? "I'm not sure about the ants, but I do know that hiding food in your room is being dishonest, and it's not healthy. If you're hungry, you eat downstairs. You don't need to hide it from me." She wasn't surprised that Katy would hide things from her mom. And if she was hiding food, what else did she think she could get away with?

She loved her niece and nephews, but she wasn't one to turn a blind eye to their faults, one of those aunts who thought they could do no wrong. She'd often said to Scott that those kids would be the death of Tricia and Mark. Look at David . . . the kid was only interested in playing video games and rarely went outside unless forced to walk their dogs.

"In fact, you never need to hide anything from me, Lyla. I'll always believe in you, trust you, and love you, no matter what. You know that, right?"

Almost every day of Lyla's life, Alyson made sure she said something along these lines. No matter what, she would always believe her daughter and stand by her side. That's what being a mother was all about.

"I know."

Alyson placed the muffin tray in the oven and poured herself some tea she'd made earlier.

"So did they come back with food?"

Lyla shook her head. "They were gone for a while though."

"How long was a while?" She really wasn't liking what she was hearing.

"Oma said not to dwell on the things that don't involve me."

Oma. That name irked Alyson more than she wanted to admit. She'd hated her own Oma. The woman had been hard and unbending, and no matter what Alyson or Tricia did, it seemed like it was never good enough.

"Do you like calling your Grandma *Oma*?"

Lyla nodded. "Oma said you grew up knowing how to speak German. Do you still?"

"*Ja.*" Alyson closed her eyes for a brief moment. "*Ich kann sie sprechen ein wenig.*"

Lyla scrunched up her face. "What does that mean?"

"I can speak it a little. I think. My German is really rusty."

"We should learn it together then! That would be fun, don't you think?"

Like stepping on broken glass. Lovely.

"Grandma . . . oops, Oma could teach us too."

Alyson's face froze with a smile she prayed her daughter didn't realize was fake.

"Sounds like a good plan, Lyla. We can start on Sundays, during our family dinners." Why now? She'd successfully erased German from their home life early on when Lyla was about four. All it had taken was a few words to her mom about how they didn't speak German at home to Lyla, so please stop confusing her, and suddenly everything was English.

"So, other than Katy and Keera sneaking out of the basement for some reason you don't know about, did anything else happen? Did you watch a lot of movies?"

Maybe it was the way her daughter's gaze skittered across the room or the moment she started to rub her fingers together, a sure sign her daughter was nervous, but everything in Alyson went on high alert, waiting for her daughter's reply.

"Lyla? What aren't you telling me? Do you know what took Katy and Keera so long? Or did you watch something that wasn't appropriate?"

Lyla started to shake her head but stopped. "I don't know," she mumbled.

"You don't know? Lyla Elizabeth Ward, you know better than that. Either you watched a video that was okay or it wasn't."

"Katy . . ." Lyla started, then stopped. She hung her head. "You're just going to be mad at me," she said quietly.

"Why would I be upset with you?" Alyson bent down and touched her forehead to Lyla's. "Remember our promise to one another? To always be truthful?"

Lyla nodded.

"Then how about you tell me what happened, and I'll try to help you fix it? Okay?"

"Okay." Lyla whispered. "Keera really likes Brandon, David's friend, so they wanted to go see what they were doing. I think he sent Keera a text to meet him in David's room."

"He . . . they . . . are you kidding me?" Keera is only eleven years old, and Brandon—he was a teenager. Okay, so only a few years apart, but still. The girls were too young for stuff like that. "And Katy went with her?"

Lyla nodded. "Keera wanted him to kiss her."

"Keera's too young to want to be kissed." Alyson couldn't believe what she was hearing. Tricia must have stopped them . . . she was supposed to keep a close eye on the kids. In fact, she promised something like this would never happen.

"She's been kissed before." Lyla said quietly.

"She has?" Kids were growing up way too fast nowadays. Eleven was too young for this stuff. Way too young.

"She said she wanted to know if a boy's kisses are different than a man's."

Alyson's world stood still.

She did not just hear what she thought she heard. She couldn't have.

"Is that what she said?"

Lyla nodded.

"No, I need to know her exact wording. Did she say exactly that, Lyla?"

Again, Lyla nodded, but this time Alyson could tell her daughter was a little frightened.

"What man, Lyla? Did she say?"

Lyla's head shook rapidly. "No. They just giggled, and then left."

"Did anyone else hear her say this? Was it to the whole group?"

"Just me. They wanted me to come too, but I said no. I didn't want to get in trouble."

Alyson closed her eyes. "God help me," she said under her breath. She couldn't believe what she was hearing.

"Then what happened, honey? What about when they came back? Did Brandon kiss her?" Could it possibly get any worse than it already was? Did her sister know? Did she realize what happened in her own house? And what did Keera mean exactly?

She knew what Keera could have meant, but she prayed to God she was overreacting.

"We started to watch some videos on the computer. First, it was funny kitten videos, and then we started to watch music videos. We all got to pick our favorite song to watch, and then . . ." Her voice faltered, and Alyson could see her struggle with her words.

"And then? Did you see something you shouldn't have?"

Lyla nodded.

"Do you want to tell me about it?" Scenarios ran through Alyson's head, and none of them were good.

"Keera picked a song that she knew the moves to, but Mommy, I didn't like it." Lyla's voice was barely a whisper.

Alyson swallowed back the bile that rose in her throat at her daughter's words. What her daughter meant, and what she was imagining were two different things. Two *very* different things—they had to be.

"And then Keera wanted to teach us the moves, but I didn't want to. Katy did though, and then Keera wanted to play a game. Where we're blindfolded, and we have to guess what she was writing on our skin with a feather."

Okay, that wasn't so bad. She remembered playing that when she was young. They would write words on a palm or on the back, and it was all so very innocent.

"But you didn't want to play that?"

Lyla shook her head. She shifted in her seat and gave Alyson a look that broke her heart. "So I went to sleep. I put my headphones in and listened to music and fell asleep before everyone else."

"Why didn't you tell your aunt that you weren't comfortable?"

"They're going to be mad at me now," Lyla said.

"They're not going to be mad at you, honey. If anything, you should be upset with them. You were there as Katy's guest. And these are your friends. Friends don't do things like this to each other. They don't place each other in uncomfortable situations." Alyson leaned in and wrapped her arms around Lyla, holding her tight.

"You did the right thing, honey. Anytime you feel uncomfortable, you leave the situation. And you tell me." She placed her hand beneath Lyla's chin and raised her face until she was looking at her. "You always tell me, okay?"

Lyla nodded, and her voice dropped into a whisper. "Can I tell you a secret?"

Alyson nodded.

"You can't tell anyone. Promise." Lyla held out her pinky, and without a second thought, Alyson hooked her own pinky inside her daughter's finger.

"Some of the dances her dad taught her, but Keera said that they were private dances." Lyla's gaze dropped to the ground, and she played with one of the measuring spoons on the counter. "And the game she wanted to play, she plays with her dad too. But she made us promise not to tell anyone, because then she would be in a lot of trouble."

"The game with the blindfold?" Alyson didn't like the sound of this.

Lyla nodded. "When Keera's dad plays the game with her . . . he writes things on her skin, and she guesses the words. There's a prize . . ." Alyson gripped the edge of the counter tight and forced herself to speak in a calm voice.

"What kind of prize, honey?"

Lyla's lips quivered before she looked up at Alyson with big doe eyes.

"Then they *do it*."

"What do you mean, 'do it'?"

Lyla's cheeks burned bright red. "You know."

Alyson shook her head. She prayed to God she didn't know. Her daughter couldn't mean what she thought she meant.

"They *do it*. Like what you and Daddy do."

"Sex? Are you sure?" It was very hard for Alyson to keep her voice calm and not freak out. Inside she was in full freak-out mode. *Ohmygodohmygodohmygodohmygod* . . .

Lyla nodded her head.

"Mommy, I'm not lying. That's what Keera said. And she was going to show us some of the moves of her dance, even though her daddy made her promise not to show anyone, and . . . I didn't like that."

Alyson hugged her daughter close. So many emotions were running through her head, through her heart . . . so many memories of things she didn't want to recall.

"Oh honey. Did she actually say her daddy does this?"

Lyla nodded.

"Thank you for sharing that with me."

"You won't tell anyone, right?"

Alyson sighed. "I have to, Lyla. This . . . what you told me, that's not okay."

"But Mommy, you promised. You can't tell. Not anybody."

"I know I did, but sweetheart, sometimes promises have to be broken if it means protecting someone else, especially when it involves a child."

Lyla frowned. "They're going to be so mad at me."

"But I'm not." She was proud of her daughter, proud that she said something, that she had come to her.

Now it was her turn to right a wrong, to do something she'd wished long ago had been done for her. Believe her and do something about it rather than turn away and pretend everything was fine.

"You did the right thing, telling me." She gave her daughter another hug. "And I'm so glad you did."

"Are you going to tell Aunt Tricia?"

Alyson nodded. She hated hearing the insecurity in her daughter's voice. "I need to, especially since this happened at your aunt's house. And Keera's mom is Aunt Tricia's best friend. I'd want her to tell me if the roles were reversed. But"—she leaned over and placed a kiss on her daughter's forehead—"I don't want you to worry about anything, okay? I'll take care of it."

"I'm not lying." Lyla whispered.

Alyson believed her. With everything in her core, she knew her daughter told the truth. Why would she lie? There was no reason.

"Lyla, I will always be on your side. Always. I will always believe you. Always fight for you and always be there to protect you. Okay?"

She'd expected to see something akin to relief on her daughter's face, but instead she saw signs of panic, of worry, and of doubt.

Alyson knew that she had to do everything in her power to wipe that doubt away. She knew what it was like to tell the truth and not be believed, to feel alone and to be betrayed by the one person who should always remain your hero.

She would not do to her daughter what her own mother had done to her.

CHAPTER SIX

MYAH

The moment they entered their home, Keera ran to her room, slamming the door so hard that the picture frames on the walls wobbled.

Myah seethed. If there was one thing she could not handle, it was slamming doors. Yell if she needed. Stomp if she had to. But never slam a door.

She wanted to race after her daughter, open the door, and demand she talk to her. She didn't care if they had to yell their feelings out until they were both exhausted . . . But instead of doing what she wanted, she hung her coat in the closet, kicked off her shoes, set her purse on the entryway table, and made her way into the living room, where she sank down on her couch and clutched a pillow tight to her chest.

When she was little, she used to scream into a pillow, something she knew Keera did as well. And given the lack of noise coming from her daughter's room, she was probably doing it now.

Things had been a little tense in the car after she'd picked Keera up from Tricia's. Myah asked them both questions about the evening, and neither one of them said much, which should have been an indication of things to come. Tricia only shook her head and then changed the subject to the dance recital, while Keera stared out the window. When they arrived at the restaurant where Eddie was waiting, Keera had ignored her and walked in to the restaurant without a backward glance.

What Myah assumed would be a casual coffee with Tricia, in the same restaurant, turned out to be something altogether different.

First, she had to hear about her daughter's shenanigans the night before. She couldn't quite believe that Keera would sneak out to meet a boy, in a closed bedroom of all places, but then she had to deal with the angry confrontation of her daughter, who approached their table saying *I hate you* loud enough for everyone in the restaurant to hear.

The moment she saw the tears streaming down her daughter's face, she knew Eddie had told her about the divorce. If Tricia hadn't stopped her, she would have let her Latina temper flare up and told her soon-to-be ex-husband where to go. Instead, she walked out, leaving Tricia alone, and went in search of her daughter. Thankfully, it was a small town, and Keera had only walked a few blocks.

The car ride home had been silent. Myah called a replacement for her dance class and tried to figure out what to say to Keera about getting a divorce.

Not once had she thought Keera would react the way she had. When she and Eddie had first separated, Keera acted like it was the best thing to ever happen . . . so why would she be so upset now?

Yes . . . Eddie had been spending more time with Keera since the separation, but not enough to form some kind of parental bond. Right?

Tossing the pillow aside, Myah decided to find out for herself.

A muffled *"What?"* could be heard through Keera's bedroom door when Myah knocked. She took that as a good sign and slowly opened the door.

Keera sat in the middle of her bed with her pillows clutched tight against her body. She scooted over so Myah could join her and willingly gave up one of her pillows to Myah.

"Are you ready to talk?" Myah asked.

Keera shrugged. Myah took that as a yes.

"I wanted to tell you myself. It wasn't Eddie's place, and I'm sorry."

"I don't really care."

Myah found that hard to believe. "So why the outburst earlier?"

Keera's chin sank into her pillow. "Because you don't care about me or my future."

"I'm sorry . . . what did you just say?"

"You don't want me to dance professionally. I get it. But Eddie sees something in me that you ignore. I think you're just doing this to hurt me."

Stumped, Myah just shook her head. Where was this coming from?

"Did you tell me you wanted to dance professionally?"

Keera shrugged. "You would have said no," she muttered.

"So why get mad at me for something I wasn't aware of? Keera . . . that doesn't make sense. I didn't think you liked Eddie? Where is this coming from?"

"I don't know." Keera shrugged.

Myah sighed and leaned her head against the wall. "Keera . . . Tricia told me about last night."

"Seriously, nothing happened, Mom. The girls were watching a lame movie, and Katy and I wanted something to snack on."

Myah's eyebrows rose. "So how does wanting something to snack on mean you end up in David's bedroom with the door closed?"

Keera didn't say anything.

"It's kind of a big deal, kiddo. You gotta give me something." Myah always thought she had a good relationship with her daughter. They were open, honest, and communicated well . . . until the last few months, when her daughter's anger seemed to be always on the surface, and she didn't talk to Myah as much.

"David and Brandon are just friends. We hang at school, so what's the difference if we hang in the room. It's not like anything happened." The defiance in Keera's voice shocked Myah.

"Of course nothing happened—Tricia heard the door closing and was there before anything could happen. But Keera, come on . . . you know better. You knew the rules, so why break them?"

"They were stupid rules," Keera muttered under her breath.

"Stupid rules or not, they were Tricia's rules, and as her guest, you should have obeyed them. You know better."

"So what are you going to do? Ground me?" She scooted off the bed and stood up.

Myah thought about it for a moment. Maybe that's exactly what she needed to do. Ground her from dance and sleepovers. She wasn't sure which one would hurt the most but . . .

"I think that's a great idea," Myah said.

"Whatever." Keera rolled her eyes. "Sleepovers are lame anyways."

Myah snorted. This from a girl who basically begged to have a sleepover every weekend.

"No dance either," she said.

"What!"

"For two weeks." Myah was glad to finally have her daughter's attention. "No classes with me or anyone else. For the next two weeks, you're not even allowed to step foot in the studio."

"That's so not fair." Her daughter crossed her arms over her chest and pouted.

"Unfortunately, kiddo, life isn't always fair. Now, I'd like you to write a letter to Tricia and apologize, and I'd like it done before bedtime." Myah left her daughter to stew in her bedroom.

Parenting wasn't always fun and games, and it was hard being a single parent. She'd hoped, with Eddie, that things would be different. But he showed no interest in Keera after they'd been married. Before? Yes. He'd been attentive and kind and made lots of promises about them being a family and him being an important figure in Keera's life, but all that changed a month after their wedding, and he'd realized that being a parent just wasn't for him.

She reached for her phone and decided to call Eddie and tell him exactly what she thought.

"Hello, love. I wondered how long it would take for you to call." Eddie's suave voice greeted her.

"How dare you?" she hissed. "You had no right to tell her about our divorce."

"I know and I'm sorry. It just . . . just happened. We were talking about her dance lessons, and I mentioned I wouldn't be seeing her as much . . . I'm sorry." The apology in his voice sounded legit, but Myah knew better.

"I don't want your apologies, Eddie. Just your respect. Going behind my back like that . . . it didn't just happen. You knew exactly what you were doing."

Something Tricia had said earlier suddenly hit her.

"You planned this, didn't you? That's why you wanted to have breakfast with her . . . for this exact reason." She hadn't believed it when Tricia first suggested it, but her friend had been right.

"Of course not. I wanted to congratulate her for last night and give her a little gift."

"A gift? You didn't mention that last night. What did you give her?" And why hadn't Keera mentioned it?

"Well, now you're just going to be mad at me for going behind your back, aren't you?"

Myah stared up at the ceiling and slowly counted . . . when she hit five, she was back in control of her emotions and not about to fly off the handle.

"What did you give her, Eddie?"

It wasn't anything big, because Keera had held nothing in her hand. She hadn't carried a purse or bag on her either, so it had to be something small.

"Did you give her money?"

"I gave her a necklace. Nothing expensive or anything, but I saw it and thought of her."

"Are you kidding me? You didn't give her a damn thing, not even your time, while we were married, but now that we're separated and I want a divorce, you're giving my daughter gifts? *My* daughter, Eddie. Remember that? The girl you didn't want to be a parent to?" She let her anger loose and tore a strip off the man who no longer claimed her heart. How dare he?

She heard a gasp from behind her, and when she twirled around, she caught Keera running back up the stairs.

"Damn you," she said before hanging up. She tossed her phone down and ran after her daughter.

"Keera . . ." she called out. But this time, instead of slamming her door, Myah heard the soft click of the door being shut, and she stopped in her tracks.

She'd screwed up. She shouldn't have said those things, not with Keera upstairs. Why did she have to run her mouth off like that?

Nothing she could say would change what she'd just said, and if she were being honest, she wouldn't lie to her daughter anyways.

But she hadn't meant to hurt her either.

CHAPTER SEVEN

TRICIA

Back from her coffee with Myah, Tricia opened the door to the garage and, poking her head in, found her husband mulling over a drawing he had taped to the wall.

"Which project is this?" She closed the door behind her and headed toward him. Snaking her arm around his waist, she too considered the drawing.

It looked like a space-age fireplace mantel.

"Don't even ask. I've been trying over the last few weeks to draft a design for something, but it's just not working." He cocked his head to the side, pulled a pencil from behind his ear, and drew a few more lines on the paper.

"Is this for a client or . . . ?"

"Nah. Just an idea I had." His attention remained on the drawing, and as she slipped away, she doubted he even noticed her absence.

"Are you hungry? Want anything? Coffee maybe?" Tricia asked, before she headed into the house.

"Maybe coffee? The stuff your mom made was nasty."

Tricia saluted, and then laughed when she realized he wasn't even looking at her. She made her way into the kitchen, listening for the sounds of the kids, and noticed the containers of cookies. She had expected Ida to still be there, but apparently, she'd already left.

She was nibbling on a cookie while the coffee percolated when the phone rang.

"Hey," Tricia said. She was a little surprised Aly was calling.

"We need to talk."

"Okay . . . what's up?" She pulled out Mark's favorite coffee mug from the cupboard, a Donald Duck mug the kids had bought him for Christmas last year, and set it on the counter.

"Myah never showed up for practice."

And this was why her sister was calling? They'd already discussed this earlier through text messages.

"I figured she wouldn't. But that's not why you're calling, is it?" She poured Mark's coffee, and with the phone tucked between ear and shoulder, she brought it to the garage, setting it down on the wood railing for him.

"No, it's not." Alyson's voice was terse.

"What's the matter, Aly?" She headed back to the kitchen and poured herself a cup—her coffee drinking knew no limits.

"Lyla had a good time, right?"

"She . . . yes, she had a good time. She enjoyed it and would like to do another one without so many kids around."

There was something in her sister's voice, something she wasn't saying.

"Yes, okay, I'll admit I might have taken on too much with all the kids. Is that what you want to hear?" Tricia asked.

"No, I want you to admit that despite keeping the boys and girls separate, it didn't work."

"Fine. It didn't work." Tricia pinched the bridge of her nose. "You did try to tell me, but either way, nothing serious happened, and it was handled." She took her coffee into her office, where she sat down in a reading chair.

"What exactly happened, Tricia?" Alyson's words were clipped, with barely concealed anger and something else . . . But why?

"Lyla wasn't involved in any way. Is that what you're worried about? It was Katy and Keera, and it's been dealt with. Lyla was perfect." Hopefully that helped to ease her sister's anxiety a little.

"Of course Lyla was." Alyson's voice softened a little. "I trust my daughter to keep her word to me."

"Excuse me?" Tricia knew an underhanded insult when she heard one.

"You heard me."

Tricia leaned back in her chair. "If you have something to say to me, do us both a favor, and just say it."

"Fine. When I came to pick up Lyla, you weren't at the house."

She knew it. "No, I wasn't. But Mom was, and considering all the other kids had already left, I figured leaving Lyla with her grandmother was okay."

"Well it wasn't. You broke your promise, and to be honest, I shouldn't be surprised, but I was. It hurt."

"Whoa." That was uncalled for. "I didn't break my word, and you . . . don't you dare even go there."

Trust was a huge issue for Tricia. She'd done everything . . . everything to protect her sister all their lives, and while she'd made a lot of mistakes, if there was anyone—*anyone*—Alyson could trust it was her.

It was a subject they'd skirted around time and again without either one actually coming out and saying what they really meant.

"Aly, I had a really long night, as you can imagine, and I'm not in the mood to deal with your . . . issues when it comes to our mother, okay?" All she wanted to do right now was soak in a hot bath before the boys came back from their friends' homes.

"Whatever. That wasn't the only reason I called." The anger seemed to disappear as quickly as it had come, and Tricia wasn't sure what to expect now.

"I don't know how to say this." She paused for a moment, and Tricia started to dread whatever her sister had to say. "I'm shocked, actually."

"Shocked? About what? Did something happen at dance practice?" Obviously, Tricia was missing something here.

"No, not at dance. At your house, last night." Alyson sounded confused. "You don't know?"

"Know what? Other than the girls sneaking off for a few minutes—"

"You"—Alyson cut her off—"apparently have no idea what happened beneath your own roof."

"What . . . what are you talking about?"

"I'm talking about the videos and dancing and . . . I can't believe you don't know." Her sister's voice broke, and for a moment, Tricia was really concerned about her sister's emotional well-being.

"Aly, why don't you come over? Bring Lyla if Scott isn't around. I'm not sure what's going on, but obviously, this is something we need to discuss in person, okay? I'm home all afternoon." She'd thought for sure Alyson had been handling everything okay. She knew letting Lyla have a sleepover here last night had been a huge deal, but maybe her sister was having a harder time letting go than expected.

"Scott will be home soon. I'll see you within the hour."

Exhaustion set in while she sat there, and she almost didn't want to move. Thank goodness her mother had cleaned up her kitchen. She could only imagine the look on Aly's face, if she'd walked in to the destruction from breakfast.

"Hey, you okay?" Mark stood in the doorway.

She shook her head and blinked away the tears that filled her eyes.

"Who was on the phone?" He bent down and reached for her hands. "Whoever it was, they're not worth crying over."

She swallowed past the lump in her throat. "It was Alyson, and I think I'm just exhausted."

"Ahh. You and me both. No more parties like that—this old body can't handle them like it used to," Mark teased as he pulled her up from the chair and fit her tight against his body while he held her. "Whatever she said to you, shrug it off."

"Something's wrong with her."

"Aly?"

"Who else." She rolled her eyes. "She blew a lid at the fact that I wasn't here when she picked up Lyla, but then . . . I think there's something else bothering her. I just don't know what." She let out a long and deep breath. "She's coming over to talk."

"My advice? Add some Baileys to your coffee before she gets here." He smiled at her. "In fact, I can make it for you, and then maybe help you relax a little?" His eyebrows wiggled at his suggestion, and Tricia had a hard time keeping the smile from her face.

"I'll take you up on the Baileys, but I should probably check in on Katy and ask her some questions about last night. Apparently Alyson thinks something else happened."

She headed downstairs, where Katy sat on the sofa wrapped in a blanket watching one of her favorite reality dancing shows.

"Hey, kiddo. I thought we were going to watch this together?" She sat down beside her daughter and pulled half the blanket over her own legs.

"Sorry. Want me to rewind it?"

"Did I miss anything?"

Katy shook her head and handed her the remote.

Tricia hit the pause button and half-turned toward her daughter.

Katy sighed. "You want to talk about last night, right?"

"I figured it might be a good idea."

"If I say I'm sorry again, will it help?"

Tricia smiled. "It always helps, but I need to know you know what happened was wrong."

"I know." She pulled her legs up tighter to her chest.

"I'm glad." Tricia placed her hand over Katy's knee and squeezed. "I thought your father and I made it pretty clear last night that what you and Keera did wasn't allowed, so I'm a little confused why you did it anyways?"

"I really don't know. Keera . . . She likes Brandon." Katy frowned. "It seemed like a good idea at the time, you know?"

Tricia shook her head. "Nope, don't know, because I'm pretty sure you both knew you were breaking the rules. Katy . . ." Tricia sighed. "The parents placed a lot of trust in me by letting there be coed sleeping in the house. They trusted me to make sure that what happened wouldn't . . ."

Katy ducked her head. "Bet you're pretty mad, right?"

"More like disappointed. You broke my trust, honey." As much as she hated to say it, it needed to be said.

Katy looked up at her with a stricken gaze. Tricia had worked hard to stress trust in her family. Trust was the foundation of everything . . . it was something she'd learned the hard way a long time ago.

"I'm sorry." This time, Katy actually sounded like she meant it. "It was stupid, and I wish . . ." She laid her head on Tricia's shoulder.

"I'm probably grounded, aren't I." It was more of a statement than a question, but Tricia was glad she'd brought it up.

"You are. No sleepovers for a while. Here or at someone else's house." She'd voted for more consequences, but Mark reminded her that since every weekend it seemed like she wanted to have someone over or go to someone's house, it might be enough. "And on weekends, you're going to have to do more cleaning around the house." She decided to add that in for good measure. That way Katy didn't think she could just watch her programs all day.

"That sucks."

"I know. So was not sleeping last night because of two girls thinking they could sneak time with some boys." She leaned her head against Katy's. "Listen, I have a question to ask you about last night, but I need you to be honest, okay?"

Tricia thought back to what her sister had said, about not knowing what happened beneath her roof. It was true, she wasn't a helicopter parent like Alyson, preferring to give her kids space to grow up without always looking over their shoulders, but she wasn't negligent.

Katy looked like she was going to say something, but stopped herself, biting her fingernails instead, a habit she'd learned as a small child.

"Katy, stop."

Her daughter pulled her finger out of her mouth and looked embarrassed. "Fine," Katy said. "I'll be honest."

"Did anything else happen last night that I should know about? Anything that I wouldn't approve of?" She had no idea what Alyson had been hinting at, so she felt like she was fumbling in the dark here. "Katherine? Is there something you need to tell me?" She pulled away from her daughter and angled her body on the couch so she was looking at her directly.

Katy shook her head. "No, Mom. *Jeesh*. We watched some videos, did some dancing, and then some people went to sleep and others played games on their phones."

"Is that it?"

Katy shrugged. "What else do you expect me to say?"

Tricia pursed her lips. "Your aunt seems to think something else happened last night."

Katy rolled her eyes. "Seriously? You're giving me the second degree here because of something Lyla said? She probably didn't like any of the videos we watched or didn't like the fact that no one wanted to watch her baby music videos." She pushed herself up from the couch. "Can I go to my room now?"

"Fine, go ahead. Your aunt is coming over shortly, by the way, and Lyla might be joining her."

Katy stomped her way up the stairs. "Just great. Like I want to hang out with her right now," she said on her way up.

Tricia wanted to say something but decided it wasn't worth the energy. She slowly followed her daughter up the stairs.

"Someone seems in a good mood." Mark said as she rounded the corner and stepped into the kitchen.

"If this is the beginning of what she'll be like when she's a teenager, then we're in trouble." She picked up her forgotten coffee mug and took a sip, grimacing when she realized the coffee was now cold.

"Aren't you glad we only had one girl then?"

"So glad. You have no idea." She slumped into him, and his arms immediately wrapped around her.

"Why don't I help you de-stress a little?" He winked.

"Oh really? And how are you going to do that?" She reached up and pulled his head down, smiling up at him.

"I'm sure I can think of a way," he said just before he lowered his head and gave her a long lingering kiss.

CHAPTER EIGHT

IDA
LATE SATURDAY MORNING

Müßiggang ist des aller Laster Anfang. Being idle is the beginning to vice. Something her own mother used to say on a daily basis. She remembered growing up hating that saying, but with her own girls, she realized how true it really was. As long as she kept the girls busy with chores or other things around the house, they were out of trouble.

For the most part. There was only so much a mother could control. Unfortunately.

"What's that you're making?" Gord entered the kitchen and poured himself a cup of coffee.

"Strudel." With all the ingredients now in the bowl, Ida began the work of hand mixing it. Strudel was a dessert that needed a personal touch, and using the new mixing bowl the girls had bought her a few years ago for Christmas just didn't do the job right.

"What's wrong?"

"Nothing. Why?" Ida worked the water into the flour mixture until a soft ball of dough formed.

"Because you never make strudel unless you're *verrückt*." Gord took his coffee and sat down at the kitchen table where Ida had placed the morning paper for him.

"Who said I was mad? I'm in the mood to bake." With the dough ready, Ida wiped down the counter and then dusted it lightly with flour.

"Uh-huh."

Ida grabbed the dough out of the bowl and dropped it hard down on the counter.

"Be careful, or you won't get any of this." Ida warned her husband. She wasn't in the mood, not after the phone call with Tricia this morning.

Okay, so maybe she was upset. But not mad. More like worried.

In order for the dough to have the right texture for the strudel, you had to be rough with it in the beginning. *Pfund es wie Sie es bedeuten*. Pound it like you mean it, her mother used to say. While everyone else in the house would disperse whenever their Mutter prepared strudel, Ida would stand to the side and watch closely. She'd count the times her mother would pick up the dough and drop it back down, and she'd notice the way her mother's body relaxed halfway through the steps, as if she worked out any issues she had on the dough.

Which is probably why Gord claimed she only made strudel when upset. It was cathartic for her.

"I heard you talking to Tricia. What happened?"

With lips pursed tight, Ida dropped the ball of dough onto the counter a few times.

"Alyson is upset." She stole a glance over at her husband and saw his frown. "She got mad at Tricia for not being there when she arrived."

"So? We were there." Gord then nodded. "I see . . . because we were there, and she wasn't." His shoulders sagged, and he shook his head in bewilderment but didn't say anything else.

He didn't need to.

"I thought with her letting Lyla stay at Tricia's . . . Why don't I call her? Maybe explain to Scott. I need to speak to him anyways," Gord suggested.

"Don't you dare. It'll only make things worse. Nothing we say or do is going to change our daughter's mind about leaving her child with us, and we both know it." She dropped the dough again. "And you just leave that boy alone. You know he works on his own projects on the weekends."

"He shouldn't have to. I pay him enough and keep him busy enough . . . He needs to pay more attention to his family."

"He has his own path to walk, just like you did," she reminded him.

Gord grunted. *"Ein weiser Mann hört auf die Älternen."*

When Gord spoke in German, Ida knew he was more than a little bothered.

"A wise man learns from his elders? You never did. Why"—a smile crept onto Ida's face—"I seem to recall you complaining about all the lectures my own father used to give you."

Gord muttered something low, and while Ida smiled, she didn't ask him to repeat himself. Her father had been hard on Gord, but then, they'd been awfully young when they married, and Gord knew nothing about providing for a wife and child. It was thanks to her father that Gord learned his carpentry skills.

"I'll talk to him tomorrow then." The table chair skidded back as Gord stood. "Call your daughter before dinner tomorrow. The last thing I want is a family argument over hurt feelings."

Ida sighed. "I'll call my daughter in a little bit. When I've calmed down."

"What's there to calm down about? This issue of hers isn't new. She'll come around one day. Just call and apologize."

"I am not apologizing for making cookies with my grandchildren. I will never apologize for being there and spending time with them." The very idea had her blood pumping. He should know better. "Besides, Tricia said she was upset about something else. She seems to think something else happened last night other than Katy and Keera sneaking off."

"Really? Is she maybe overreacting as usual?" her husband asked.

Ida shrugged. "Your guess is as good as mine."

"Fine," Gord grumbled. "Who's hosting the dinner tomorrow anyways? Sure hope it's not Aly's turn. I don't ever want to taste that cauliflower crap she tried to pass off as mashed potatoes again."

"Tricia's." Every Sunday afternoon, they alternated homes for their family dinners.

"Gonna be a madhouse then."

Ida nodded. It amazed her—the difference between her two daughters. Tricia's home was chaos and noise and loud love. Aly's home was serene, clean, and while not quiet, it was manageable.

"You know what? Don't you think it's time to stop giving Alyson the white-glove treatment? Both you and Tricia tiptoe around her as if she's made of glass and you're afraid she's going to shatter if you stand up to her too much."

"I . . . I do not," Ida sputtered before picking up the dough and slamming it down onto the counter. By now, the dough was becoming smooth and stretchy, just the way it should be for strudel. "I do not tiptoe around my daughter," she finally said through clenched teeth.

"You do. You always have. Ever since she was little and—"

"Enough!" Ida yelled, stopping her husband from saying anything more. "Enough," she repeated, but this time with her voice lowered. "You've made your point. Now go, and leave me be. Don't you have a cabinet or something to make?"

Without thought, she began to knead the dough, pushing with her clenched fists one way and then another, the rhythmic motions helping to calm her down. She knew Gordon was still there, standing behind her, but she ignored him. She counted the seconds, continuing the process for a full minute before she shaped the dough into a disk. She reached for the oil and spread it on top, smoothing it on with her fingers before putting the dough in a bowl and covering it with a cloth.

By the time she prepped the filing, the dough would be ready.

"Why are you still here?" She finally turned, hands on hips, and glared at her husband, who smiled at her. She ground her teeth with frustration.

"I love you." He held out his arms.

"Verrückter alter Mann." You crazy old man. Ida let out a long breath. "I love you too, you old fool. Now scat. I've got work to do and don't need you distracting me."

She lifted her head and accepted his kiss.

"Now go, or I'm never going to get this made." She swatted at his arm and watched as he sauntered off to his workshop.

"I don't tiptoe around Aly," Ida mumbled to herself, while she gathered the washed apples from her sink. "You make it sound like I'm afraid of my own child and that's the furthest thing from the truth. I just respect her boundaries, that's all."

To prove her point, she reached for the phone and called her daughter.

"Mom, now isn't a good time," Alyson answered.

"Sounds like it might be the perfect time then. What's the matter?" For once, she'd like to be there for Alyson, really be there and have her daughter see it, accept it, acknowledge it.

"If I tell you, you won't believe me, so I'm not going to waste my breath. I'll talk to you later, okay?"

"No. Wait." The words rushed out from Ida, worried that Aly would hang up on her. "Tell me. Let me help."

Alyson snorted—the sound harsh and unforgiving. "Trust me, there's nothing you can do to help." Ida recoiled from the bitter ring in her daughter's voice.

"Tricia mentioned—"

"Tricia mentioned what exactly?" Alyson interrupted her. "Seriously, does she need to go running to you all the time? If you're calling to talk about my conversation with Tricia earlier, don't. That's between me and her."

"Now that's enough." Ida didn't like where this was going or how Alyson was talking about her sister. "I don't understand where you get off thinking it's okay to act this way with me. I'm your mother, and you can show me some respect. Whatever you think happened probably didn't, but as usual, you're blowing it out of proportion."

The moment she said the words, Ida knew she'd gone too far.

"You don't believe me—surprise, surprise. Why did I even think you would? I should know better by now. Do me a favor. Leave me alone right now."

"Aly, that's not what I—"

There was a click on the other end of the phone. Her daughter had hung up on her.

"Meant," Ida finished. She groaned in frustration. Why couldn't she say the right things at the right times, rather than messing it up?

She continued to slice the apples before adding the pieces to the bowl and coating them with cinnamon sugar. Something was wrong with Alyson, and she prayed it had nothing to do with Lyla. Alyson had her own demons, and hopefully, that was all it was.

Hopefully, it wasn't anything worse. Ida didn't know what she would do if history was repeating itself.

CHAPTER NINE

ALYSON

For the umpteenth time, Alyson checked the time on her phone. Scott was supposed to have been back ten minutes ago. He always called or sent a text if he was running late, and so far he hadn't.

What could he be doing? Where was he? This wasn't like him at all.

Exactly three minutes later, she heard the garage door open and she breathed a sigh of relief. She waited patiently for him to walk into the house, having already poured him a cold glass of water and set out some cubed cheese and pepperoni sticks for him to snack on before he walked up the stairs for a shower.

"Thanks, hon." It was the first and only thing he said once he walked in the door. He downed the water, and bit into the cheese, and then he visibly relaxed.

"Where's Lyla?" He looked around the room.

"Upstairs in her room." She'd been up there for the past forty-five minutes. "We need to talk, but I know you want to shower first, so—"

"Can I hurry up?"

She gave him a nervous smile. "If you don't mind. I need to run over to Tricia's, but I wanted to talk to you first."

"I'm not that sweaty. I can wait." He grabbed the remaining snacks she'd laid out for him and sat down on a stool beside her. "What's going on? Did something happen? Is Lyla okay?"

"She had fun at the sleepover, if that's what you're worried about, but things happened last night that I'm concerned about."

Alyson filled him in on what Lyla had told her, about the two girls sneaking out of the basement, about the videos and the dancing the girls took part in. At first, Scott's concern was focused on Lyla . . . Was she involved in any way? How did she feel about the videos they watched? But when Alyson stressed the things Lyla told her . . . the things that Keera apparently said, his face blanked, and she knew he understood her concerns.

"She actually said she wanted to know if a boy kissed like a man?"

Alyson nodded.

"How would she know? Why would she say something like that?" He leaned forward and rested his elbows on the counter. "That doesn't sound like Keera at all."

"That's not all."

"There can't be more." Scott pulled back and ran his fingers through his hair, causing strands to stick up.

They cared a lot about Keera. Gordon liked to call Keera, Katy, and Lyla the three musketeers. They were always together.

"Apparently there were videos the girls danced to, but some of the dance moves Keera did were . . . they weren't things Myah had taught the girls in class." She really wasn't sure how to explain what Lyla told her.

"Okay, that I believe. Both her parents are dancers, so of course she knows things the others don't. Right?" Scott asked.

Alyson considered this. "Perhaps. But apparently Eddie has been giving Keera private lessons."

Scott's eyes widened as the understanding of what she was saying hit him.

"Have you talked to Tricia?"

"That's why I'm going over. Well, that and something else too. When I went to pick Lyla up this morning, Tricia wasn't home. It was just my parents." She winced as she realized how pathetic her anger had been.

"Pick your battles, Aly, please? Lyla probably had a lot of fun with your mom and dad, right?"

She nodded. "She did. They made cookies, and she brought some home for tonight. I already got in an argument with Tricia about it," she admitted.

Her husband shook his head at her. "You know how I feel, Aly."

"And you know how I feel." She wasn't going to argue with him about it. Not now. They had bigger issues to deal with.

"What do I do about what Lyla told me?"

"Talk to your sister, and see what she has to say. She was there . . . maybe Katy or another one of the girls said something. I'm assuming all the girls heard what Keera said, right?"

Alyson didn't know. It wasn't something she thought to ask Lyla about, but she would need to.

"If what Lyla says is true—"

"If?" Alyson cut him off. "She wouldn't lie about it."

"Of course she wouldn't. But what if Keera . . . exaggerated? As much as I hate to say it, but what if? You don't want to do something or say something if it's not true." There was a note of caution in Scott's voice.

"I don't think Keera would lie about that. She's too young to say stuff like that for attention . . . right?"

"I don't know." Scott stood up. "Kids are maturing a lot faster than we did now. Just . . . promise me you'll talk to your sister first before doing anything?"

"Of course I'll talk to Tricia."

"First." Scott reiterated. "Promise, Alyson. Figure it out with your sister. She knows Myah best, and there's no need to overreact when there might not be anything to react to."

Alyson swallowed a reply, but only because she knew he was right. She did have a tendency to jump first when it came to children and anything that looked suspicious.

"No child deserves to be hurt like that, Scott. You know how I feel."

He laid his hand on her shoulder. "You're very passionate about protecting those around you. It's one of the things I love most about you." He leaned forward and kissed her forehead.

"Heading over there now, then?" he asked her.

She nodded. "I'll be back soon."

She watched him walk up the stairs and thought about his comment—about not overreacting. As much as she tried not to let it, it hurt to hear him say that.

She thought of the time when she'd volunteered as a class mom in Lyla's kindergarten class, and one of the boys had come to school covered in bruises and wearing the same soiled clothing nearly every day. All signs of abuse to her—or so she'd thought. She'd had no idea the family was on welfare, but then, if it hadn't been for her, no one would have known just how sick the boy had been. Turned out he had hemophilia, a clotting disorder . . .

She wasn't overreacting this time. She knew it in her heart. She believed what her daughter told her and knew it was crucial to do something about it. Kids just didn't say things or play games like Keera wanted to play . . .

The thought of it made her sick to her stomach. No child deserved to be hurt like that—no child.

CHAPTER TEN

MYAH

Myah's fingers trembled as she dialed her best friend's number.

"Hey, you okay?" Tricia answered immediately, thank God.

"I'm . . . Tricia, he . . . I can't even . . ." She sighed. "No, I'm not okay." She stood at the base of her stairway and looked up.

"What's going on?"

"Can you talk for a moment?" Myah asked her. When she said yes, Myah made her way to the front porch, gently closing the door behind her, and sat down on the steps.

"I messed things up in a bad way." Her chest felt like it was about to rip open. "I called Eddie after we got home and . . . well, things didn't go well. He bought Keera a necklace to celebrate the dance recital, and it got a little heated, and I said some things . . ."

"Things that probably needed to be said. Don't beat yourself up about it." Tricia's voice was soothing, calm, but it didn't help much.

"Keera was listening."

"Oh."

"Yeah. *Oh.* I didn't say anything that wasn't the truth, but . . ."

"But it wasn't a truth your daughter needed to hear, right?"

"Exactly." Myah let out a long sigh and dropped her head.

"Do I need to guess what you said? The fool could have cared less about your daughter while you were married, so why now? It doesn't make sense, Myah."

She knew her friend would understand, knew Tricia would get it.

"That's basically what I said, just more. I should have . . . I didn't even notice . . . but then I had no clue either . . ." She couldn't gather her thoughts, let alone complete her sentences.

"I didn't think Keera liked him. What changed?"

Myah sat up and leaned back until she was looking up at the sky. "I have no idea. But apparently not only does she hate me, but she texted Eddie and told him she hated him too, which led him to call me back . . . and Tricia, the second call didn't go so well either."

"You need to take that girl's phone away," Tricia mumbled.

"I know." She should have done it right away, especially after last night.

"What did he say?"

"He threatened me."

"I'm sorry—he what? Why?" Tricia sounded as confused as she felt.

"I don't know." Myah tried to keep control. She swore that she would not let one more tear fall because of her ex-husband, and she meant it.

"Tell me exactly what he said."

Myah glanced behind her to make sure Keera wasn't at the door. "He said if I kept Keera from him he was going to destroy me."

"What? Are you kidding me? What is wrong with him?"

"He said he'll ruin my reputation and destroy what we've built with the dance hall if I attempt to destroy the relationship he's working so hard to build with Keera."

"Is he going through a midlife crisis or something? Wait." Tricia remained silent for a moment. "Do you think this has anything to do with her dancing? Does he think that she's his second chance maybe? His big comeback? If he can't do it with his own dancing, maybe he can coach someone who can?"

The thought had occurred to Myah, and this was exactly what she didn't want to happen.

"He says she wants to dance," Myah admitted.

"But she's your daughter. Has she told you that? I wouldn't believe anything that comes out of his mouth." Tricia's disdain for Eddie was no secret. She'd told Myah not to marry him. She'd told her buying the theater with him was a mistake . . . and she should have listened to Tricia. But Myah thought she knew him better— after all, they had been dance partners for years. She knew and accepted him for all his flaws and thought they could make it, that their love for each other would be enough.

She'd been wrong. Very, very wrong.

"I don't know what to do, Tricia. I don't understand this need for him to have Keera in his life. I don't get him at all. Before we were married, he liked her, liked to do things as a family, but once we got married, it was like he didn't care at all about her, like she was in his way . . . but now . . . and to threaten me . . . what is wrong with him?"

"Should you bring it up with your lawyer?" Tricia asked.

"I don't know—should I?" Good question. Legally, he had no right to her daughter, no say in her life or anything else.

"Myah, if he's threatening you, then yes, I think so." There was some background noise. "Listen, my sister is here. I'll call you later, okay? But don't panic. We'll figure out what's going on and what to do, I promise."

Myah did feel better after talking with Tricia.

She knew she needed to go back inside and talk to her daughter, figure out what was going on and discuss what happened at the sleepover. It was times like this she hated parenting. No one warned you about the preteen years, the puberty and hormones and how hard life could really be when you're a single parent.

She learned early on to pick her battles with Keera . . . but this battle, she had a feeling it would turn into an all-out war, and she had a feeling Eddie was the one to blame.

CHAPTER ELEVEN

TRICIA
SATURDAY AFTERNOON

"Want to help me fold towels?" Tricia asked as she opened the door for her sister. She caught the quick smile from Aly and knew she'd made the right choice. Give them something to do, something to concentrate on, while Aly said whatever it was she came to say.

As kids, Ida used to send them to the laundry room to fold or sort clothes when they had issues to work out.

"Scott made it home?" It was probably a good idea that Lyla didn't come. Katy was still up in her room, and her mood probably hadn't improved yet. Tricia led the way into the small room and set the towels down.

"I know I'm a little late, but I figured it would be best if I came alone."

Neither sister said anything, but Tricia gave her sister a smile as they both began to fold towels together.

"You had something you wanted to tell me? If it has anything to do with the fact that I went out for coffee with Myah and left the kids alone with Mom and Dad, I'm not going to apologize." She stopped short, surprised at her own words. She'd meant to say she was going to apologize . . . right? "I mean . . ." She let out a frustrated sigh. "Listen, it's my house, and I trust—"

"Have you talked with Katy yet?" Alyson interrupted her. From the lack of expression to what she'd just blurted out, Tricia almost wondered if Alyson even heard her.

"Of course I did."

"And?"

Tricia dropped the towel she held. "And what? What am I missing here? Other than my daughter and Keera sneaking out, it was an average sleepover party. Just with more kids than normal."

"You consider what went on, normal?" Alyson dropped her gaze to the towel she was folding. "What exactly did Katy tell you happened?" She said quietly, as if processing her thoughts and filtering her words.

Tricia rubbed at the spot on her wrist that always seemed to ache when she was tired or stressed, and unfortunately right now, she was both.

"Why don't you tell me what you're concerned about first?" she suggested.

"I don't even know where to start."

Alyson took another towel to fold, and when Tricia noticed her trying to form the right words, her stomach dropped.

"Just spit it out."

"According to Lyla, the girls were watching videos and were going to play a game before bed. A game that involved one girl being blindfolded and . . ." She stopped, looking behind her to the hallway.

"And what?"

Alyson sighed. "I think you need to talk to Katy. And Tricia . . . I think there's something you need to know about Keera."

"Alyson? If you know something I don't, then you need to tell me."

"I think . . . I think Keera's been sexually abused by Eddie." The look on Alyson's face as she said this . . . Tricia knew she wasn't joking.

Keera abused? Why would Alyson think that? And Keera seemed fine both last night and this morning. If she'd been abused, Tricia would know.

"Why would you say something like that?"

"Because of what Lyla told me this morning."

"Are you sure? You've been wrong before and . . . Katy said Lyla fell asleep pretty early last night." The moment she said it she knew she shouldn't have. But there was no way Alyson could expect to drop a bomb like she had and not expect Tricia to be off balance right now.

"I'm sure." Alyson's gaze didn't waver.

"The girls were watching music videos, and I guess the ones Keera picked were quite . . . suggestive. She knew all the dance moves and said Eddie had taught them to her."

"Well of course he would have. He is a dance instructor too. What would you expect?"

Alyson shook her head. "These aren't dance moves you teach a ten-year-old, Tricia."

"You can't claim a child has been sexually abused just based on dance moves."

"I'm not. She also mentioned a game she played with a man. A game no girl should *ever* play. Ever. Come on, Tricia. I know what abuse looks like. I'm not making this up." She took in a deep breath, her body shuddering from the force. "But this is Keera. *Our* Keera." The rigidity in Alyson's stance softened, and she looked at Tricia with a pleading gaze.

It was the way she said *our*, with the heartbreak and despair in her voice, as if it were one of their own daughters.

Tricia shook her head. She thought back to all the times Keera had been at her home, from before the divorce until now, and no, she couldn't believe it. Alyson might know what abuse looks like, but so did Tricia. She also knew what it looked like when you were trying to hide it from others, and Keera didn't act like that. She wasn't secretive, exhibiting or concealing her body. She wasn't overly forward with men or acting scared . . . She was a normal ten-year-old girl.

Except for . . .

"Lyla wouldn't lie to me."

"I never said she did." Tricia cleared her voice. "But this . . . you do understand what you're saying, right?"

"I'm fully aware. Why do you think I'm here talking to you about it?"

Tricia reached her hand out and touched her sister on the arm. "But just me, right? No one else? Not yet?" She needed to make sure. Her sister had cried wolf one too many times in the past.

"I'm really worried, Tricia." The softness of her sister's voice, the finality of her words . . . it brought back feelings Tricia wanted to forget.

"I need you to tell me everything Lyla said. Everything."

"It started with music videos. The girls were dancing, showing off their moves. Lyla said they each picked a song, taking turns. But Keera's choices were inappropriate."

"What do you mean, *inappropriate*?"

Alyson blinked a few times. "I'm using Lyla's words here. Moves that Myah won't teach them in class, things that ten-year-old girls shouldn't be doing. But then Keera told them Eddie had taught her these moves."

Tricia nodded. Okay, that sounded . . . plausible.

"That's not all." Alyson crossed her arms over her chest. "Lyla told me that before the girls sneaked out last night, Keera said she wanted to see if a boy's kisses were different than a man's."

"She wouldn't have said that." She didn't want to believe it.

"She did."

Tricia thought about her conversations with Myah and how off Eddie had been lately. Could it be true? But she would have seen the signs. Myah would have seen the signs.

"They also played a game." Alyson kept going. "Another one that Keera said Eddie played with her but couldn't tell anyone."

Tricia's heart sank, and she leaned back against the wall.

"Talk to Katy, please."

"Of course I'm going to talk to my daughter. But is there more you're not telling me? You can't just come over here, claiming something like this without . . ."

"All I know is Keera made the girls promise not to tell. But Aly . . . it's not okay. This is Keera. Kids that age don't just dance like that or play those types of games, Aly. They just don't."

Tricia shook her head. "What kind of game exactly?"

"Something about being blindfolded and touching each other's skin."

"Oh, Alyson. Don't you remember playing those games when we went to sleepovers as kids? We'd write on each other's backs, and you'd have to guess the word?"

Tricia was taken aback by the glare from her sister.

"Lyla told me Eddie rewarded Keera for guessing right whenever they played this game. I'll give you one guess on that reward, and no, Tricia, it wasn't a lollipop." Alyson's lips thinned.

"We both know how I feel about Eddie, but a child abuser? Having sex with Myah's daughter? He's a sleazeball, but not like that." Tricia swallowed hard. Her sister was on edge. She could see it in the way her body vibrated with . . . anger? "Let me talk to Katy. Find out her side of the story, and if I think it's anything, then I'll talk to Myah, at least let her know that her dancing is probably not age appropriate."

"I can't believe you." Alyson said between clenched teeth.

"Are you 100 percent sure?" Tricia reached out and lightly touched her sister's hand. She needed Aly to calm down.

"Maybe you should have a talk with your daughter and find out exactly what happened. Find out about the videos and the dancing. Then ask about the game where Keera brought a blindfold." Alyson's nostrils flared. "Games like that happen for a reason." Her words were measured, short, and clipped. "Ask her about the comment Keera made about kissing boys."

There was a moment of silence between them.

"Oh, Alyson." Tricia looked at her sister with sympathy, her heart saddened for the worry and fear Alyson must be experiencing right now.

Their past hung over both of them like a wet wool blanket, but instead of moving forward and living in the present, Alyson let it rule her life and lived in constant fear.

It was why she was so controlling with Lyla, why she rarely left her side and kept her daughter dependent on her rather than teaching her self-reliance.

But Alyson knew what it was like to be the victim of sexual abuse. They both did.

"We don't want to see those signs," Alyson said softly. "We don't want to be watching our children to see if we've missed something, if we failed to protect them. I think, as mothers, we're sometimes the last to see it. So does Myah know? Probably not. But she needs to."

"And you're going to be the one to tell her?" Tricia didn't like where this was going.

"If I have to. But I think you should."

Tricia caught the look of determination in her sister and knew if she didn't do something now, Alyson would leave her and head straight for Myah's house. She couldn't let that happen. She couldn't. She needed to calm down, think logically, and get her sister to meet her at least halfway.

And by halfway, she meant not do anything irrational. Because if there was one thing she knew, when Alyson had her mind set on something, she went full steam ahead and made sure it was done.

"Okay." She breathed in deep. "Let's take a step back. You're right, if something happened, we need to deal with it. But first, I need to understand . . . She specifically said Eddie had taught her the dances and the games and sex was the reward?" Tricia needed to be sure.

"Those are my words but you get the idea."

"I do. But here's my issue. Katy said nothing about any of this when I talked to her. Nothing. And I don't see any signs from Keera that we should be worried." Tricia thought about her conversation with Katy earlier. She'd talk to her again, just to be sure, because she did agree, Lyla's version of events did raise red flags.

"I can't believe this. I really can't. I know what Lyla told me."

"What are you accusing Katy of exactly?" She rubbed her wrist and inhaled deeply. She needed to remain calm.

"I'm not accusing her of anything."

"That's not what it sounds like, Aly."

Alyson's gaze lifted. "I didn't appreciate Lyla being in a situation she wasn't comfortable with. Katy knowns Lyla isn't allowed to watch those type of videos, and that game . . ." Alyson said. "I'm not accusing her per se, but I am concerned. Worried even. It's not natural, Tricia. Can't you see that?"

"They are ten-year-old girls, Aly. This is the age they're going to start testing their limits, of what they are allowed to do and what they can get away with. Don't you remember doing that? You're making this out to be more than it is."

Alyson shook her head. "I'm not."

"Then she exaggerated." No matter what her sister thought, Lyla wasn't the little angel she professed to be. She couldn't be. Sure, she was innocent and extremely sheltered, but she'd seen the look in her niece's gaze when her mother wasn't looking, and she was ten. No ten-year-old was perfect.

Alyson's face blanched.

"I thought you, of all people, would understand. That you would want to make sure your daughter was protected and safe. That you can be so blasé about this . . . that your daughter's innocence may have been stolen from her . . ." Alyson stopped, as if unable to finish her thought.

What? How did this go from being worried about Keera to suggesting something had happened to Katy?

"Trust me, if anything had happened to my daughter, I'd scare even the devil, but nothing did. I think . . . I think we both need to calm down, take a deep breath, and think things through."

Alyson shook her head. "I can't ignore this." Alyson crossed her arms over her chest and frowned. "This isn't . . . it's not okay."

Tricia sighed. "You're right, it's not. So let's figure out what we can do about it, okay?"

"Talk to your daughter."

"I will." Tricia agreed. "What about Keera? No child should have to go through something like that. You and I both know that better than anyone."

A haunted look crossed through Alyson's eyes.

"I know," Tricia said softly. She was worried, but not for her daughter. For her sister.

"If you don't talk to Myah, I will." Alyson said.

"No, I'll talk to her. Let me find out what Katy has to say, and then I'll talk to Myah. Just give me some time, okay? I will call you once I've spoken to her."

Alyson stared deep into her eyes, as if trying to see through her words, to see if she was telling the truth or not. Eventually she seemed satisfied with what she saw, and after giving her a quick hug, she left.

After she said good-bye to her sister, she realized it had been this time of year that their world had fallen apart, that their innocence had been taken from them. A heaviness settled on her, and she rubbed the area on her wrist even more than normal. No wonder Aly was on edge.

"Everything okay?" Mark followed her as she made her way up the stairs to the bedroom with the basket of towels.

Tricia shook her head. She started to say something but couldn't, and tears fell instead. She dropped the basket and sat down, covering her face as a range of emotions coursed through her. Mark sat beside her and gathered her close.

"Whatever it is, it's going to be okay," he whispered into her ear.

Tricia leaned into his embrace and struggled to contain herself. This was ridiculous. She didn't fall apart like this, not after all this time.

"I know." Tricia hiccupped. "Alyson just . . . she just . . ." She couldn't even say it. She breathed in deep, steadying herself before she pushed herself up and wiped the tears from her face.

She kept her gaze down, embarrassed that Mark had caught her crying. She hated crying. It was a sign of weakness, and Tricia was anything but weak. She didn't fall apart like this, didn't lose herself in her emotions, didn't allow herself to go back to those dark days when all she'd wanted to do was disappear.

Mark didn't say anything, and for that, Tricia was grateful. She stood up and gathered the towels and placed them in the closet in the hallway, and by the time she returned to the bedroom, she felt calmer, more in control.

"Are you ready to talk?" Mark still sat on the bed, waiting for her.

"Alyson thinks there's a lot more that happened last night than just the girls sneaking out to see the boys."

"More as in . . . ?"

"You don't want to know." Tricia shook her head.

"Tell me."

"Did you notice anything this morning, anything odd between Katy and Keera? Or anything odd about Keera for the past few months?" Mark, despite being a guy, was pretty observant when it came to their children. If she'd missed anything, he might have picked up on it.

He shook his head. "Other than the extra whispers?"

"There was a lot of that, wasn't there? Probably girl secrets or inside jokes." Her stomach twisted. Girl secrets? Was it possible?

"What does that have to do with your sister?"

"Alyson thinks that something happened at the sleepover—something that shouldn't have happened."

Tricia proceeded to fill Mark in on what her sister had told her, as well as what was going on with Myah and Eddie. It felt good to talk it through, to see if there were any connections.

They both sat there, and a heavy silence permeated the room.

"We need to talk to Katy."

Tricia jolted to her feet. "I'll do it."

"I was going to work on that fireplace mantel some more. I don't need to be here." With puppy-dog eyes full of fear, he looked up at Tricia. "You don't need me here, right?"

"I've got this." She hoped she had this. Except she had no clue how to handle this at all.

Tricia headed to her daughter's room, where she found Katy lying on her bed, headphones covering her ears while she watched the latest episode of *Step It Up*, the latest dancing show for young teens, on her tablet.

"Hey, Katy?" She closed the door behind her and sat down on the bed, close to her daughter's feet.

"What's up, Mom?"

"Can we talk?"

"This isn't about last night again, is it?" Katy rolled her eyes.

"I need to ask you a question."

"Okay." Katy sat up and turned the power off on the tablet, and set her headphones down around her neck. "What's up?"

"We've talked before about protecting our bodies and knowing when something is wrong. Right?" She waited for Katy's nod and ignored the confused look in her eyes. "Did anything . . . odd happen last night that shouldn't have?"

"Um, no."

The look on her daughter's face said only one thing—*What is wrong with you?*

Tricia sighed. "I just need to ask one more time about the videos and games. You guys behaved, right? Is there anything you might have forgotten to tell me earlier? Like . . . watched something you shouldn't have or played a game that—"

"No, Mom." Katy rolled her eyes. "We didn't play board games. We did the usual sleepover stuff."

Tricia latched on to that. She understood sleepover stuff.

"Like what? Truth or dare?" Please let that be all they played—
and a clean, childlike version of it.

Katy shrugged. "Something like that."

Tricia's heart sank. Maybe Alyson was right after all.

"Was anyone blindfolded while playing a game?"

Katy's eyes widened before she shook her head. "No. Why
would you ask that?" Katy jumped up from the bed and headed to
her closet, where she grabbed a sweater and pulled it on.

"You cold?" Tricia asked. She eyed her daughter, who was wearing jogging capris and a tank top.

Katy shrugged before she sat back down, folding her legs
beneath her.

"So there were no blindfolds involved in any games played?"
Tricia asked again, changing the words slightly to make sure her
daughter understood the question.

"No, Mom. No blindfolds. Seriously, why would you even ask
that?"

Tricia studied her daughter and felt okay with her answer. So
okay, no blindfolds. Was anything else about Lyla's story true then?
Should she push harder to find out if there was more, or just trust
that Katy spoke the truth?

"What about the videos though?"

"So we watched some videos."

"Did you watch any videos that were improper? And I'm not
talking about just for you, but for Lyla as well." She gave her daughter a pointed look. She realized the girls were ten, but what was
appropriate for Katy was not always okay for Lyla, as sad as that
was. In fact, Tricia doubted if Alyson even let Lyla watch music videos unless they were the Wiggles or something meant for preschool
children.

Katy shrugged. "Knowing Lyla, probably. It was like everyone on my music list and stuff."

Tricia let out a long breath. This she could handle. She knew Katy's music list because she downloaded the songs or albums for her. And it was true that at least half of the songs Alyson would not like Lyla listening to.

"Did you guys dance and stuff?" There was a smile in her voice because she was trying to picture her girls doing dance routines in the small bedroom.

Katy nodded. "We practiced some moves from class, and then Keera showed us some her parents had taught her. She wasn't sure if she should, because . . . well, because of Lyla. But honestly, she needs to learn to handle this stuff. You know?"

"I get it. I do. Want to hear a story?" She started to laugh at the memory that came to mind and couldn't wait to see how her daughter reacted.

"When I was young, probably a few years older than you, I used to play these games at sleepovers where we'd see how far we could push ourselves or each other. And we'd tell stories. In fact, that's when I first learned a friend of mine had had sex with her—"

"Stop!" Katy covered her ears with her hands and groaned. "Please, we are not talking about that right now. How gross can you be?"

She leaned over and gave her daughter a hug. "Sorry," she said as she squeezed. "Kittens and unicorns, that's what we used to talk about." She chuckled as Katy's face bloomed bright red.

"You're so weird," Katy said.

Tricia breathed in deep before she placed a soft kiss on her daughter's forehead. "I know. Mom's tend to be like that." She squeezed her daughter again before letting go.

"Your dad is in the garage. What do you say you and I go raid your father's chocolate stash he tried to keep hidden in the mud-room and then watch a movie? I think I saw one saved on the DVR from last week you wanted to see."

Katy shook her head. "His stash is empty. I already checked. And I watched that movie already and deleted it."

"What?" His stash was empty? Since when?

"Yeah, I checked last night. All that was in there was an empty wrapper and a note."

"What was on the note?"

Katy started to giggle.

"What's so funny?" Tricia narrowed her gaze as she tried to think about what the note could say. Knowing Mark . . .

"It said, *Check Mom's closet for her secret stash. Large black purse behind wedding dress. I'm all out.*"

Tricia groaned before shooting to her feet and heading toward her closet, with Katy close behind her.

He wasn't supposed to have known about that spot. He'd found all her other ones, but this one was new. Or newer at least. And yet, when she pulled back her dress and reached for the purse, she knew right away he'd not only found it but emptied it.

She looked inside anyway and found a note. She didn't need to pull it out to read what it said since it wasn't folded.

Gotcha.

CHAPTER TWELVE

IDA
SATURDAY AFTERNOON

Ida walked past the crowded grocery store parking lot and made her way toward the quaint downtown core where her favorite deli, produce, and bakeshops were located.

She'd left Gordon at the Legion to meet up with his friends before dinner and play a hand of cards, or whatever it is he does there. It keeps him happy, out of her hair, and gives her an hour of freedom. She'd join him for dinner there, as they did every Saturday evening before heading home to watch something on the television while she knitted. She liked routine, and their Saturday routine was just fine.

She pushed open the door of the deli and was assaulted by the loud voice of Gunther Erhard, the owner of the deli, talking to another customer in German.

"Er dachte das Fleisch im Supermarkt sei Müll." He thought the meat at the grocery store was garbage. It was one of his favorite subjects—comparing his supplies to that of his brother's store next door.

"Ratet mal wo die Frau meines Bruders ihr Fleisch kauft? Me. Ha! Was hat das wohl zu bedeuten?" Guess where my brother's wife buys her meat? What does that tell you? Gunther pounded his chest.

"It tells me she understands the value of small business owners in our town," Ida spoke up. She liked Hilda, Randolf's wife. "Randolf understands the importance as well, and you know that."

Ida perused the meat selection and thought about maybe trying something new rather than sticking with her regular order.

"You'll try the sausages. It's a new recipe, and Gordon will enjoy the garlic I added." As if Gunther read her mind, he'd already pulled out four sausage links and set them on the scale to be weighed.

"I'll get my usual too," Ida said.

"Of course you will. Did that old man of yours stay home today?" Gunther had his back turned while he was packaging up her meat and cheese.

"I dropped him off at the Legion."

"Men like us, we don't retire. He needs something to do, not waste his time there playing cards and drinking beer. I've got a project for him if he's interested. Are you heading to the Legion for dinner or shopping a bit?"

"Shopping."

Gunther nodded and placed her bag in a cooler behind him, on the bottom shelf. "I'll keep this for you then. Make sure to tell Gordon what I said. Remember, I close on the hour."

"I'll let him know." She paid, and then took the slice of meat he offered as a little snack. She waved good-bye before heading down the street to her next destination.

She was going to the café at the end of the street but decided to stop in at a little novelty store full of knickknacks and antiques. There wasn't really anything she needed, but she had the time to waste, and she never knew what she'd find in the store.

Claudia Teering stood on a small ladder, an apron wrapped around her waist, and was dusting the books that ran along the top shelf.

"Don't you have a granddaughter or a worker who can do that for you?" Ida stood there, watching her old friend dust, and frowned.

"I'm almost done." Claudia smiled at her, gave another twirl of the duster in her hand, and then carefully made her way down the ladder. "It's a slow day, and I need to keep busy," she said before giving Ida a hug. "If I'd known you were coming in, I'd have put on a pot of tea."

Ida glanced around the store. "I thought you closed up your tea spot after the summer?" In the far back, Claudia had set up some tables and chairs and offered fresh baked goods she'd bought from the bakery down the street as well as tea.

"I decided to open it on the weekends for a few loyal locals." She winked at Ida, who instantly felt guilty because she had planned on heading down to the café for a cup of tea and a scone.

"Do you have time?" Claudia asked.

"Of course." She followed Claudia. "I'm just going to look around while you get the tea ready."

"Take your time," Claudia said. "I had a new shipment come in from my cousin down east. She sent up some good finds." Claudia pointed to a shelf off to the side, so that's where Ida headed.

She casually looked at the antique pots, bowls, and glasses but didn't see anything that caught her eye, so she browsed the rest of the room before heading toward the back, where Claudia dished up scones and set out two cups of tea.

"How about that recital last night?" Claudia's granddaughter was also in Myah's dance class.

"It was very sweet." Ida couldn't have been more proud of her girls than she had been last night.

"I spoke to Sarah this morning after the sleepover—sounded like she had a good time." Despite her words, there was a look on Claudia's face Ida knew all too well.

"And?" If her friend had something to say . . .

"I heard about the escapades as well."

"Well, I'd be a little surprised if you hadn't since Sarah was there. But she wasn't involved, so let's keep the gossip to a minimum, shall we?" Ida knew her tone was brisk, but too bad. The last thing Tricia needed was gossip to spread like wildfire.

"Ida, no need to be like that with me. I don't gossip about our families." Claudia pursed her lips before she took a sip of her tea, and Ida could see the hurt in her friends gaze.

"Sorry, I just . . ." She shrugged.

"No need to explain, and you're right. Sarah wasn't involved, which was a good thing, because she would have been in a lot of trouble. Kids these days," Claudia tsked. "We wouldn't have had the nerve to pull that nonsense when we were kids."

"No, but then, we didn't have sleepovers like they do now either." Ida agreed with her. Parenting had become far too relaxed. Kids got away with more than they should, and parents didn't exert the authority they used to.

And kids were better for it, were they? Not in her book, they weren't.

Ida's cell phone rang in her purse, and as she pulled it out, Claudia rose. "I'll give you some privacy," she said as she left.

Ida glanced at the screen of the phone the kids insisted she keep on her. It was Tricia.

"I was just talking about you," Ida said to her daughter. "Little Sarah had fun at your house last night according to Claudia."

"Oh, good! I'm a little worried I'm going to start getting angry phone calls or e-mails from parents."

"I'm sure you won't. Stop worrying about it so much." Tricia was very much like her. She didn't focus on the things that didn't matter in the long run and didn't worry about every little thing that came her way. Worrying did no good.

Tricia sighed. "I need to worry about it, Mom. I wish I didn't. Alyson just left . . ."

"What does Aly have you worried about now?"

"She thinks Keera is being sexually abused by Eddie."

Ida gasped. She couldn't help it.

"Sorry, I should have warned you," Tricia said. "I begged Aly not to do anything or say anything until I find out for sure, but you know Aly."

"I'm going to call her," Ida said. She needed to do something to stop her daughter from making a fool of herself and from hurting another family with her false accusations and her own insecurities. "Why can't she just leave things alone?" she moaned.

"That's not the Aly way," Tricia said softly. There was a smile in her voice, which Ida caught. It was a saying they'd created when Aly was just a child. She had always been stubborn and difficult and determined to get her own way, all the time. *Not the Aly way* was a saying everyone repeated, from her teachers to her friends . . . even now.

"Your father is playing cards at the club. Why don't I just go and stop by her house before I pick him up? Have a little talk with Alyson and find out what's going on," Ida suggested.

"Are you sure that's the smart thing to do?"

Ida heard the caution in her daughter's voice, but she ignored it.

"Of course it is. She's my daughter after all. Hopefully, she'll listen or at least talk to me." Things weren't always the best between them, but they weren't bad either.

"Okay," Tricia said. Ida could hear the relief in her voice. "Let me know how it goes. Call me after, okay?"

Ida hung up and gathered her purse before heading to the register and putting some money down on the counter.

"Claudia, I need to run and talk with Alyson. Thanks for the scone and tea. I'll come back next weekend for another pot."

Without waiting for a response, Ida left the shop and made her way back down to where Gordon had parked their car. She glanced at her watch and realized only a half hour had passed, which left plenty of time for her to talk to Aly before coming back for her husband.

Plenty of time, hopefully, to talk some sense into her daughter before she did anything foolish, like telling someone who mattered that Keera had been abused by Eddie, of all people. The man was full of himself for sure, but he'd never hurt a child. He wasn't that type of man.

CHAPTER THIRTEEN

ALYSON
SATURDAY EVENING

Alyson was in the kitchen prepping for dinner, when the doorbell rang. She quickly dropped the onion she was about to peel, wiped her hands on her apron, and rushed to the door. It had to be Tricia with an update.

She'd been on pins and needles all afternoon waiting for her sister to call or text about her conversation with Katy. They needed to form a plan, discuss the next steps. God forbid Keera was out with Eddie right now . . . Her stomach clenched at the idea, and she pushed it aside. There was no way Tricia would let that happen. She'd call Myah first. She knew she would.

She opened the door prepared to see her sister on the other side, but it was her mother.

"What's up?" she asked as she opened the screen door to allow Ida in.

"We need to talk." Ida stood there, purse clutched in her hands, and frowned.

"I'm in the middle of getting dinner ready." Alyson turned and walked toward the kitchen, assuming her mother would follow, but in reality, not caring in the least.

Her mother wasn't one of her favorite people, for a lot of reasons, but normally Alyson managed to hide how she felt, or at least, she thought she did. But right now, all her emotions were at the forefront, and she doubted she could hide anything if she tried.

"Can I help?" Ida asked.

Alyson shook her head and pointed toward the table. "I've got it, thanks."

She took a moment to breathe deeply—she knew she needed to relax. Taking her frustration out on her mother wasn't the right thing to do. So she uncorked a bottle of red wine and poured herself a glass.

"Would you like some?"

Ida shook her head. "I won't be here long. Your father is waiting for me at the Legion for dinner."

Alyson took a sip of her wine, letting it settle on her tongue for a moment before she swallowed. "What do we need to talk about, Mom?"

Ida's face morphed into a look Alyson knew all too well.

"Let me guess," Alyson said before her mother could start. "Tricia called to talk, or maybe to ask your opinion, as a good daughter would, and you decided that you needed to come and talk me down, to stop me from doing anything drastic—again." She took another sip of her wine and watched the way her mother's eyes widened. "Am I close?" She couldn't keep the sarcasm out of her voice if she'd tried.

"You don't need to talk to me with that tone. What have I ever done to you to deserve your condescension?" Ida asked. "No, don't answer that." She stopped Alyson with a wave of her hand. "I'm well aware of what you think gives you the right, but for once in your life, can you stop reacting as a child and act like the adult you're supposed to be." Ida stood up and stepped to the counter, facing Alyson.

"Everything I have done in my life has been to protect you, to help you . . . as best as I knew how. Condemn me all you want for falling short, but remember one thing: everything you do for your daughter, I did for you." Ida gripped the edges of the counter, and for the first time in a long time, Alyson saw the hurt in her mother's eyes. "It may not have been enough, but it was all I could do."

"Mom, I'm sorry." Ida was right. Of course she was right. "I thought I'd dealt with everything a long time ago, but it's times like this, when I know something is wrong, that it all comes flooding back. I can't ignore it, I can't push it down deep into that well like you and Tricia seem to be able to do . . . I try, but I can't."

"Maybe it's time to go back to counseling?"

Alyson was shocked at Ida's suggestion. In the beginning, when Alyson first started seeing a psychiatrist, her mother had scoffed at the idea.

"It helped you before. Maybe it will help you now. I know you feel Keera is being abused by Myah's husband, but until you know for sure, I think you need to take a step back. That's why I'm here."

"I don't need to take a step back. Why would I? I'm not making up what Lyla told me."

"I don't think you are. I didn't mean it to sound like that. But . . ." Ida shook her head and looked away.

"But what?" Alyson prodded.

"Do you remember what happened with that mother's group you used to attend when Lyla was just a baby?"

Alyson grimaced. She'd forgotten about that.

She'd joined a local moms' group where they met for an hour a few times a week at different homes—it was a chance to get to know other young moms, let their kids socialize with other children, ask for advice . . . and develop some good friendships. On a day when it was Alyson's turn to host, she'd caught two little boys, the ages of two and three, in the bathroom with their pants pulled down and with the two-year-old on his knees. Shocked at what she saw, Alyson asked the boys what they were doing. The boy who was three said his daddy told him it felt good, so they wanted to try it.

Alyson had flipped out, caused quite the stir at her house, and ended up calling Child Protective Services on the parents of the three-year-old boy.

What Alyson thought had been sexual abuse turned out to be a little boy who'd woken up in the middle of the night and saw something his parents never intended him to see or hear.

"I remember," Alyson said. "But this is different. I know it is." She had no doubt, not after the things Lyla told her. "But I'm not rushing into anything, I'm waiting on Tricia, for her to talk with Katy and find out for herself."

Relief washed over Ida's features until she gave her daughter a sharp look. "Are you sure? Or are you just saying that to placate me?"

Alyson sighed. "I'm a grown woman. I don't need you to check in on me or give me permission to do what I know is best."

"I realize that." Ida hitched her purse over her shoulder. "But I wanted to be sure that you weren't going to do something foolish."

A moment of guilt flashed through Alyson's mind. The accusation of being a child abuser doesn't go away just because it turns out to be untrue.

"I wouldn't do that to Myah, not unless I was sure."

"We all need to be sure."

"I don't need you to be sure of anything. This doesn't concern you at all, in fact. It involves my daughter and her friend and my sister since it happened at her house. I don't need you to give me permission to do anything, Mother." She could feel her body begin to shake with stress and took a deep breath. "Thank you for coming over, for giving me your advice. But I didn't ask for it—so don't be too upset if I don't follow it."

She picked up the knife on the counter and cut the onion she'd been ignoring in half. The sound of the knife hitting the cutting board filled the room with a thud.

After a solemn pause, Ida took the hint and walked out of the house.

Alyson set the knife down and held up her trembling hands. She needed to calm down. One thing she'd learned through counseling was that she allowed her mother too much power over her emotions.

She picked up her glass and, in one swallow, drank the rest of the wine before filling it up again.

All throughout dinner, the only thing Alyson could think about was the situation her mother had mentioned earlier. She couldn't even remember the names of the parents involved, but she would always remember the guilt she'd felt afterward when she'd found out the truth.

She'd placed a spotlight on a family that didn't deserve it and ruined their reputation in the process.

Her father had a saying. *Die vergangenheit wiederholt sich immer, aber wir sehen es nie kommen.* The past always repeats itself, but we never see it coming.

There was a niggling piece of doubt—it was small but present—that maybe she was overreacting. Maybe she was looking for more in a situation than was actually there.

But then she would remember the words Lyla said. *Does a boy kiss like a man?* Why would Keera say something like that unless she would know? And the seductive dance moves . . . Yes, it was completely plausible that what Alyson considered inappropriate others might not. Especially Eddie, whose life was dancing, but . . .

With Lyla in bed and Scott in the other room watching television, Alyson sat in her reading chair in the study, phone in hand, and debated whether to send Rachel a text asking to talk. Or she could just wait.

"Having second thoughts?" Scott stood in the doorway, startling Alyson.

She'd talked to him while they were cleaning up the kitchen, and while Scott listened to all she had to say, he also cautioned her to wait. But what if by waiting, Keera continued to be hurt?

"I wish Tricia would call me." She hadn't responded to any of her texts, e-mails, or phone calls. That could only mean one of two things: she was leaving it in Alyson's hands to deal with, or she had no good news.

"Don't do anything tonight, okay? Sleep on it. Think about it a bit more. There's no rush," Scott said.

No rush? What was he thinking? What if it had been Lyla?

"Someone needs to protect our girls." If no one else would do it, then she would.

"Whose job is it to protect Lyla?" Scott asked.

"Ours." She knew where he was headed with this. "And don't even go there."

His eyebrow rose at her remark. "I wouldn't have to if you'd stop letting your past dictate your present." He rubbed his face.

"Aly, I know you trust our daughter, but . . ." He shook his head and didn't finish his sentence.

"Talk to her tomorrow after dinner. That's all I ask. Okay?" He stared at her, willing her to promise him something she wasn't sure she could do.

She gave him a side-glance and a halfhearted smile while mentally praying that he'd just leave her alone.

Either he heard her or God answered her prayers, because the next thing she knew, he turned and walked away. "Want coffee or a glass of wine?" he called out.

"Wine." What was the harm with one more glass? Besides, what she was about to do wasn't for the faint of heart. "But I'll come and get it," she called back to him. The last thing she wanted was for him to return and continue his crusade to get her to wait.

She pushed herself up from her chair and went toward the kitchen, when her husband stopped her. He held a bottle of her favorite wine in one hand and a glass in the other.

"I said I would come and get it," she said.

He nodded. "I know. I also know you only said it to get rid of me."

"Not true."

"You'll do whatever you want to do, and nothing I can say or even do will stop you. I know that." He held out the wineglass to her.

He knew her so well. "So now what?"

"So now"—he twisted off the wine stopper—"I pour you a glass of wine and remind you that no matter what, I'll always have your back—whether I agree with you or not." He poured wine into her glass and once it was half-full, he replaced the stopper and leaned forward, giving her a kiss.

Alyson took her wine and sat back down, bolstered by his support.

She did know best.

She hesitated for a few seconds before typing her text.

Rachel, this weekend something happened, and I need to talk to you about it. Can we meet for coffee in the morning?

She hit send and tried to relax. At least Lyla was okay. Her daughter was okay. She would do everything in her power to ensure her daughter *never* had to go through what she did.

Her memory of what happened that afternoon when she was a young teen might be fuzzy, but she knew . . . she knew deep in her soul . . . that her innocence had been lost, that she'd been abused, and no one had believed her. Except for her sister. She'd been the one to come into the room while . . . *he* . . . was there. But not even her own mother had believed her, not even when Alyson had broken down in front of her, sobbing in the corner of her bedroom. She could remember, however, the scowl on her mother's face, the way she left the room, her shoulders stiff, hands clenched at her side. She recalled the shame she'd felt when she had to repeat her story to the neighbor next door, the mother of the teen who'd taken advantage of her. She knew what it was like to be called a liar, to have her words doubted, and to become a pariah.

She breathed a sigh of relief as the weight of her decision eased. Yes, she'd meet Rachel in the morning, but they'd just chat. She wouldn't say anything. She'd wait. She'd talk to her sister and see what Katy said. If need be, the two of them, her and Tricia, could talk to Myah together.

It was the least she could do, dealing with this together, after everything Tricia had done for her.

She rinsed her mouth out and then stared at herself in the bathroom mirror, watching as the stress around her eyes eased. An old saying her mom used to tell her came to mind. Sie *können nicht allen retten, aber wenigstens diese eine.* You can't save everyone, but you can save the one. Her mom used to tell her she carried the world on her shoulders, and it was true. It always had been true.

"You okay?" Scott knocked on the bathroom door.

"Yeah, I'm okay now." She gave him a smile as she came out.

"I'm proud of you," he said. "I'm glad you didn't contact Rachel. Her being the principal of the elementary school means she's going to look at this as a school safety issue."

She sighed. "Well, I did, but only to talk to her as a friend, and I trust her. I think it will be okay. If not . . . well, either way, I'll talk to Tricia tomorrow and go from there."

Scott reached for her hand and entwined his fingers with hers. "How about a little hubby time then? Lyla is in bed reading a book, and there's a movie coming on we could watch together."

Watching a movie was really the last thing she wanted to do. She'd rather take a long hot bath and read one of the books sitting in the pile on her bedside table. But, the idea of sitting with Scott and cuddling up beside him swayed her.

"Is there any wine left?"

"Enough for a refill. Why don't you go make us some of your awesome popcorn, and I'll get your wineglass from the office." He winked, the dimples in his cheek appearing.

Alyson shook her head. "Once Lyla smells that popcorn, she'll be out of bed wanting some. How about I make you a waffle sundae instead?"

When Scott's eyes lit up, she knew she'd picked the right snack for him. She had enough of the frozen yogurt left in the freezer.

"You're trying to seduce me, aren't you?" Scott teased.

Alyson chuckled and shook her head at him. "No, but I really appreciate you standing by me in this—even if it turns out to be nothing."

The look on his face told her everything she needed to know. He believed it was nothing, that she was overreacting . . . but despite all that, he still stood by her.

And that was the basis of their marriage right there.

CHAPTER FOURTEEN

IDA
SUNDAY MORNING

"Das ist Bescheuert." Ida fumed as she listened to Tricia on the phone. Ridiculous. She couldn't believe what she was hearing.

"What's wrong?" Gordon placed his hand on her shoulder and squeezed, but she shrugged him off.

"We'll deal with it as a family. The way it should have been handled in the first place," Ida said to her daughter. She didn't bother waiting for a reply and just hung up, slamming the phone down on the counter.

"Bescheuert. Bescheuert," she muttered, so mad she couldn't think of any other words to describe what she'd just heard. "That daughter of ours . . ."

"Which one?"

Ida filled a glass up with water and headed toward the dining table, where she sat down and smoothed out the tablecloth she'd ironed earlier this morning.

"Alyson." Ida shook her head, not really wanting to say out loud what her silly daughter had done. "I need to get the roast in the oven. Tricia is coming over early with the kids."

"The roast can wait. You're agitated, and I don't like it. If you don't calm down and figure things out before the kids get here, we both know what will happen."

Ida snorted. "I don't know what you're talking about."

Gordon pulled out the chair next to her and sat down. "Tell me what happened."

Ida sighed.

"Alyson blew something out of proportion, and now everything is about to explode. Or so says Tricia."

"I don't understand."

Of course he wouldn't. She hadn't told him about what happened at the sleepover or even the events that unfolded yesterday. So she filled him in, giving him the bare bones, knowing he could fill in the missing pieces on his own.

"I don't understand it. Why would she do something like that? Why would she talk to Rachel when it's a family issue? Family laundry does not get aired in public. Ever," Ida said as she finished. Tears welled up, and she squeezed her eyes shut to stop them from flowing down her face. "Doesn't she realize what she's done?"

"Why does our daughter do the things she does? Fear. Plain and simple. She is afraid," Gordon said at last.

"But why?"

He shook his head, unable to say the words both of them thought.

This was a topic they never discussed—the past. The time when they lived on Wellington Street, in that small little cottage where her favorite roses bloomed and where their girls had been born. From the time *that family* moved in beside them until the following year when they moved to their current house—well, they lived as if that period never happened. It was better that way.

"You going to talk to her?" Gordon asked.

Ida shook her head. "Tricia asked me not to. Said she'd deal with it."

"At least tell her to wait until after dinner. I'd like to eat in peace. It's the least we deserve in our old age. We can take the kids out for ice cream after, and they can yell and scream at each other all they want." Gordon got up. "I'm making tea. Want some?"

"Don't you think it's a little too early for tea?" As much as she enjoyed a pot during the day, when Gordon made tea, he always added a little bit of whiskey, but he normally waited until the evening.

"When is your daughter coming over?" The look Gordon gave her was part dismay and part sarcasm—priceless.

"Our daughter"—she emphasized *our*—"will be here shortly. If you're talking about Tricia."

Gordon filled the teakettle with water. "Then I'd better get started. And I think you should join me."

Goose bumps ran along Ida's forearms and up her back. Yes, she probably should join him.

CHAPTER FIFTEEN

ALYSON

By the time she returned home from her coffee with Rachel, Alyson's whole body shook. She walked past Scott and Lyla, who were watching a renovation show together, and walked up the stairs and drew a bath.

It seemed like it took forever for the heat of the water to permeate her bones and warm her up.

What had she done? She laid her head back and closed her eyes.

The coffee shop was busier than Alyson had expected this time of the morning but then, she shouldn't be surprised. The café was located across the street from the town's sports complex, where Lyla was at her swim practice.

She nodded at a few of the other moms who were in here and pretended not to see their surprised glances.

She was a firm believer in supporting your child in whatever activity they were in and that included being at all their practices.

She'd even been a bit vocal about it, which explained the looks she was getting.

She could count on one hand the number of practices she'd missed, whether they were swim or dance. Even missing today's had been a struggle, but it was the only time Rachel could meet her.

She waved to Rachel, who was bundled up in her coat and scarf with her hair in a messy bun as she walked in. Alyson had managed to snag a corner table away from the others so they wouldn't be overheard or bothered, and she had sat there for the past five minutes or so thinking about what she was going to say.

"Thanks for meeting this morning. I'm sorry your day is so rushed." She gave Rachel a hug before they both sat down.

"Thanks for the coffee." Rachel wrapped her hands around the warm mug and inhaled.

"Half sweet, coconut milk. Right?"

Rachel nodded and took a sip. "Perfect. Have you tried coconut milk yet?"

Alyson shook her head. "It was hard enough to get Scott switched over to almond milk."

"Try it for yourself. You'll like it. If you can use coconut oil in your cooking, you can drink coconut milk, trust me." Rachel sat back in her chair, sipping her coffee with a smile on her face.

They sat there, sipping their coffees and smiling at one another until Alyson couldn't take it anymore.

"I need your help."

At her words, Rachel set her coffee cup down and straightened her back. She looked Alyson directly in the eye. "I'm here."

From out of nowhere, tears welled up in Alyson's eyes, and she gave her head a quick shake.

"Aly?" Rachel leaned forward and touched her hand.

"I'm okay." She smiled weakly. "I'm okay," she repeated, as if to reassure herself.

"Whatever it is, I'm here, okay? God knows, you've been there for me enough. What can I do to help? Just tell me? Is it Lyla? Scott? Your parents?"

"Something happened this weekend that really scared me. Before I tell you, I need two things from you." She waited for Rachel to nod. "I need you to listen to me all the way through, and I need you to listen to me as a friend, not as a principal. Okay?"

Rachel leaned back slightly. "It depends on what you're about to tell me. If it places me in a situation where my ethics could be questioned . . ."

"Please, Rachel? I need your help." It was very rare for Alyson to admit she needed anyone's help, and truth be told, she wasn't sure what she'd do if Rachel said no.

"Tell me."

Alyson swallowed and, faltering only a few times, she managed to get the story out. About the sneaking out, about how Lyla felt uncomfortable with the videos and the dancing, and then she began telling Rachel about Keera's comment.

Alyson lay awake all night thinking about all the possible scenarios, why a ten-year-old girl would say the things Keera had said, wondering if she was making too much out of it, remembering how she'd done so in the past . . . her insides were all torn apart from it all.

"It's the anniversary of . . ." She choked up. "Of when—"

"I know. I remember." Rachel leaned forward and placed her hand over Alyson's. "That's actually what I thought you wanted to talk about."

"Keera sneaked out to see the boys because she wanted to know if a boy kissed like a man." She pushed the words out, not taking a breath, needing Rachel to hear what she had to say. "She said her father had taught her some dance moves and some games. But the games were sexual, and she was sharing this with both Katherine and Lyla and—"

"Stop." Rachel released Alyson's hand and sat back in her chair. She planted her hands on the table and shook her head, all sympathy and understanding erased from her face. "I can't hear anymore. You can't tell me anymore." She held up her hand as Alyson opened her mouth. "I mean it, Aly."

Rachel stood and gathered her purse. "You've placed me in a situation that's not fair. Talk to me about your past, about what you went through, and I will be there for you as a friend 100 percent. But the moment you bring a child into this and suggest . . ." She squeezed her eyes shut. "Oh Aly."

Alyson sat there, stunned at Rachel's outburst. "I don't understand."

"I know." There was a sadness in Rachel's voice. "If there was any doubt about how you feel, any doubt about what you were about to say, you wouldn't be talking to me. But I think there isn't any. I think you know in your heart that what you were about to tell me is true, and that's why you asked me to meet you. Because you knew I would have to act. Legally, I have no choice." She took out her phone. "There were a lot of girls at that sleepover, Alyson." Rachel sighed. "Lyla, Katy, and Keera, right? Anyone else that I need to talk to?"

Alyson shook her head. "I don't think so. Lyla only overheard the conversation between Keera and Katy because she sat beside them. What are you going to do?" There was a knot the size of a lime in her stomach as she realized what she'd just done. Was Rachel right? Had she gone to Rachel knowing she'd have to do something?

"Can you come in to the school before first period tomorrow? I'll send you a calendar request once I know what time." Rachel's fingers danced along the screen of her phone while she talked. "I'll have to have Tricia bring Katherine in and then Myah and Keera. I'll need to hear from the girls themselves what happened before anything else." She frowned. "And of course, I'll need to bring Child Protective Services and the police in on this. I'll call Debra Jacobs."

"The one from the restaurant the other night?" This wasn't what she wanted. "You don't need Lyla. I just told you her story." Her hands shook at the awareness of what she'd just done.

"Exactly. *You* told me. We'll need to hear it from Lyla herself." Rachel placed a hand on Alyson's shoulder and squeezed. "I know that's probably not what you wanted to hear. You probably wanted me to look into Keera's story, but what if it's not all you think it is?"

"But—"

"Or," Rachel interrupted her, "what if it's more?"

The bathwater was growing lukewarm by the time Scott came in. "What's wrong?"

She quickly wiped the tears from her face. "I don't know," she whispered, unable to sort through all her emotions.

Scott knelt down and reached for her hand. "It's going to be okay."

A cold shiver ran along her body. "You don't know that. What if I just made things worse? Will Myah ever forgive me?"

"We'll cross that bridge if we have to. Together," Scott said. He leaned over and kissed her forehead. "Why don't you get out of the bath, and I'll put on a fresh pot of coffee before we head over to your sister's place. Lyla is making brownies for dessert—I picked up a mix yesterday and thought I could make them with her." He smiled. "We're even adding chocolate chips to it."

"I could have made it from scratch you know. It would taste better."

His eyes twinkled as he shook his head. "I'm in the mood for the really-bad-for-you-but-tastes-oh-so-good kind of brownies today." He reached for the towel she'd laid on the counter and placed it to the side of the tub where she could reach it. "See you downstairs."

Alyson listened to Scott whistle as he headed down the stairs and then smiled when she heard his voice.

"Let's make some fudge brownies!"

Alyson climbed out of the tub, her movements slow as she went through the steps of drying off, rubbing lotion over her body, and then getting dressed. She almost didn't want to go for dinner tonight, thought about calling it off . . . It was rare that anyone did that unless a child was sick, but she wasn't sure she wanted to face her sister or her mother.

By now, both Tricia and Myah would have received a phone call or e-mail from Rachel. Tricia was going to be livid, feelings of anger and betrayal no doubt running rampant. But what was she to do? She'd ignored her texts and e-mails, not to mention phone calls.

She still firmly believed she'd done the right thing. But now she worried about the ramifications and everything that would follow. Rachel wouldn't waste time on this, not when a child's safety was at risk.

And a child's safety was at risk. That's what she needed to remember. It would be worth it if it meant protecting Keera.

CHAPTER SIXTEEN

TRICIA
SUNDAY AFTERNOON

Tricia paced the floor of her kitchen. Mark had already herded the kids down into the basement with her father, which left her and her mom alone.

"Beer, whiskey, or wine?" Ida sipped at her tea, and Tricia knew from the way her mother's eyes twinkled that the tea was spiked.

"Beer." She opened the fridge and took out a *doppelbock*, a type of German beer her father always brought with him.

When these dinners were at her house, her mother always took over, and truth be told, Tricia didn't mind. The kitchen became her mother's domain, and Tricia was just there to help out.

"Have you talked to her yet?" Ida asked.

Tricia shook her head. "Hasn't been a good idea so far."

"You need to calm down before she gets here."

Tricia snorted.

"I mean it. I won't be having you both arguing or ruining a perfectly good meal over this." Ida set her tea down and headed to the sink full of potatoes.

"I think this is more important than a roast, don't you?" Since when did her mother care about ruining a good meal? Growing up, meal times were loud, raucous affairs—her parents would argue back and forth about the littlest things, and more often than not in German.

"What I think is that your father and I are getting old and can't handle the stress anymore. That's what I think." Ida sighed as she began to scrub the potatoes and then set them in a bowl.

"You're just afraid of how Alyson will respond, aren't you?" She watched the way her mother kept her head down, unable to look her in the eye and knew . . . she knew . . .

"Oh my god, Mother. You can't be serious? Alyson is not some frail child anymore. She's a bloody adult."

"Don't you swear at me." Ida's shoulders stiffened, and Tricia threw her arms up in exasperation.

"So sorry." She picked up a knife and potato and began chopping.

"The skins need to come off."

"Let's try something new for a change." She continued to chop the potato into small pieces before throwing them in a pot.

They worked in silence, Ida cleaning while Tricia chopped, until she couldn't stand it anymore.

"You do realize what's she's done, right?"

Her mother nodded. "I do."

"There's no going back. None. What if she's wrong?" Tricia's grip on the knife tightened. Ida reached over and gently placed her hand over top of the knife, and Tricia let go. The knife dropped into the sink, and Tricia let out the deep breath she'd been holding in.

Getting upset with her mother wasn't going to solve anything. She needed her mom on her side. She needed an ally when she confronted her sister.

"No, you're right. She has no idea. She's reacting out of fear, when she should have talked to you first. But getting upset with her won't help anything—you and I both know that."

"Stop making excuses for her." Tricia shook her head.

"I'm not."

"You are. You always have. We both have. All this family has done is try to shelter her, to keep her safe when we should have made her face the truth. She thinks she's so strong, but she's not." Clarity hit Tricia so hard she almost reeled back. She was just as much to blame as the rest of her family.

"I hope you're not placing all of this on your father and I—"

Tricia reached out and rested a hand on her mother's arm, stopping her. "Of course not. We've all done it." She leaned her head back, staring up at the ceiling. "We're all to blame," she whispered.

"Tricia . . ." Her mother leaned forward, elbows on the counter. "I don't even . . . I just . . . I want my family to be safe. To be happy. That's all I've ever wanted."

Tricia didn't know what to say, so she just nodded. Things happened to their family years ago that they never fully recovered from, and it seemed like today was the day of reckoning.

"Whatever you do"—Ida went back to washing the dwindling mound of potatoes in the sink—"please don't let it tear this family apart. Speak to your sister, get her to see what she's done, and try to fix it. Please?"

Of course she would. That's what she did—fixed things for her sister, even if Alyson never saw it that way. She'd lied to her all those years ago, never once admitting the truth to her.

There were secrets upon secrets within their family. What was one more secret?

She knew what her mother was asking. No matter what actually happened to her daughter or between their daughters, her mother wanted the truth hidden, swept under the rug. It was easier that way. Easier for Ida.

"Hey, Mom?" Katy appeared in the kitchen. "Um, Opa wants to know if there's more tea." Her gaze dropped to the floor.

Tricia knew she must have heard part of the conversation. But how much?

"Of course he wants his tea," Ida mumbled beneath her breath and reached for the cup Katy held in her hand. "He should come out and get it himself rather than send you for it. Go tell him that." She shooed Katy out of the kitchen and shook her head. "What is he thinking?"

"He's probably too scared to come in here. I'll take it to him." Tricia waited for her mother to pour the tea and add the whiskey. "Leave the rest of the potatoes. I'll be right back."

She took the tea and headed down the stairs, careful not to spill any of the hot liquid on herself, not surprised to find her daughter waiting for her at the bottom.

"Why are you and Oma arguing?"

"We're not." Tricia sighed. "We just . . . see things differently, that's all."

Katy crossed her arms over her chest. "That's not what Opa said."

"Oh really?" Tricia's eyebrow rose at her daughter's stubbornness. "And what exactly did your dear Opa say?"

"That war was brewing, and he knew better than to find himself enlisted." Katy shrugged.

"Unfortunately, your Opa is already involved, whether he likes it or not." She smiled at her daughter, hoping to alleviate the tension she saw in Katy, and walked past her into the room.

"I've never known you to run from a fight." She smiled down at her father while handing him his tea.

"Not running. I just know when to retreat and when to advance. Today there's no victory in advancing."

"Angsthase." She just called her father a scaredy-cat.

He only shrugged before taking a sip of his tea.

She turned but hesitated halfway up the stairs, eavesdropping on the conversation her mother was having with Alyson, who must have just arrived.

"Oops." Scott hesitated at the top of the stairs. "Didn't see you coming up. Sorry," Scott said.

"No worries. Everyone is downstairs, as I'm sure you know." Tricia tried to smile back, but hearing her sister's voice brought back all the rage she'd felt earlier. "I didn't expect you guys to show up so soon."

"Aly wanted to come."

"Hey, Aunt Tricia." Lyla appeared behind her father.

"Hey, honey," she said as she climbed the remaining stairs to give her niece a hug. "Did you have swim practice this morning?" She fingered Lyla's damp braid, which hung over her shoulder. "Why don't you go down and see the others. Opa has a football game on, but I think the boys are wanting to play a game."

She watched as both her niece and brother-in-law walked away before she stepped forward and into the kitchen.

"Hey, Tricia. I brought some wine." Alyson stood there, holding a wine bottle out toward her.

"Is that a peace offering?" Tricia asked.

"Mom just asked me the same thing." Alyson set the bottle down on the counter.

"Why did you do it, Aly? Why did you have to tell Rachel?"

"Tricia . . ." Alyson swallowed and struggled with her words. She reached out, but Tricia shook her head.

"No. I don't want excuses, just the truth. Did you think it would be a good idea, that once you told Rachel, all your fears would go away? Did you even once stop to think about Myah?"

"I didn't mean to . . . well, I did, but I wanted to . . . I wasn't expecting . . ."

"What do you mean, you didn't mean to? Did you or did you not meet with her this morning with the sole purpose of telling her about the sleepover? And did you not tell her about Keera and your fear that she'd been abused sexually?"

"Yes, I did. But it's not what you think. She's my friend. I needed to bounce something off of her. I needed to talk through my fears and find out if it really was just me." She sighed. "You all think that I'm just projecting this, that I'm living in the past and letting it overshadow everything else, and I needed to know."

"So you had to ask your best friend who is also the principal of the school our girls go to? What were you thinking Alyson?"

It was time to stop protecting Alyson, to stop soothing her or walking on tiptoe around her. She'd screwed up big time, and it was all Tricia could do *not* to freak out on her.

"Tricia." Her mother warned her.

"No." Alyson stepped up. "She's right. I wasn't thinking. Rachel basically said the same thing too. It doesn't change anything though," Alyson said.

"Excuse me? This changes everything. Everything, Alyson. Don't you get that?"

"I do."

Tricia shook her head. "No, I don't think you do. Not really. Did you think about Myah at all? Did you think about how she's about to get broadsided with this, thanks to you? And what about our kids? Did you think about what this is going to do to them?"

"I get it, Tricia. I do. But Keera is one of our own, right? If she's not at your house, she's at my house. Our girls are growing up together. What if I'm right? What if?" Alyson blinked away tears that gathered in her eyes.

"We need more information before we make accusations. That's the point, Aly."

"That's enough," Ida interjected before she picked up Tricia's discarded knife and began to chop the potatoes. "You girls can be nice to one another or take this conversation elsewhere. But I warn you, if you leave, you'll regret it." She gave them both the *mother stare,* and Tricia backed down. For now.

"Now, these potatoes need to get on the stove, and the last thing I need is your father grumpy because dinner isn't ready in time. So why don't you pitch in and help?"

Tricia grabbed the ingredients for a salad out of her fridge.

There was an edge to the silence in the kitchen while the women worked.

"Aly? Everything okay? Your father sent me to check things out and make sure you're all still in one piece." Scott stood in the kitchen doorway.

Alyson shook her head, Ida held her knife up, and Tricia . . . well, she was tired of keeping quiet, of keeping the peace or putting others ahead of herself.

"I got a call from Rachel," Tricia told him.

"I figured as much," he said, looking at Alyson.

"You know, Keera rarely sees Eddie unless she's at the theater," said Tricia. "And last night? She was at home with her mom. How do I know? Because I texted Myah and asked. Yes, I thought of it, Alyson. But instead of jumping the gun and overreacting, I wanted to get the facts first. And I was going to meet with Myah tomorrow and talk to her about this. But now I can't." Tricia's shoulders sank.

"Why couldn't you have just waited, Alyson? You should have given me time."

"I did. If you had answered my text messages and e-mails, then I wouldn't have—"

"Seriously? You're going to place the blame back on me?"

"Whoa!" Scott interrupted. "I think we all need to sit down and discuss this. Does Mark know?" Scott asked.

"Yes, get out of the kitchen," Ida muttered.

"Mother . . ."

"What?" Ida turned to Tricia, tears in her eyes. "Let me work in peace while you figure this out. As a family. The way it should have been handled from the beginning." Ida clenched her lips tight.

Scott called down the stairs for Mark. He came up the stairs and stood talking with Scott, and while Tricia couldn't hear what they were saying, she got the drift when she heard Mark swearing.

When Mark stomped into the kitchen, a murderous look on his face, Tricia sat down at the table, folded her hands together, and waited for the explosion. She knew it was coming, had known all morning that he would do this—he needed to do this. Mark rarely got upset. He was a carefree guy who let everything slide off his back, unless it involved her or the kids.

"What were you thinking?" Mark clipped his words tight, his fists clenched at his side as he looked from Alyson to Scott and then to her.

Tricia swallowed. "Mark . . ."

"Getting upset isn't going to do any good." Tricia rubbed the ache that flared in her wrist while trying to calm her husband down.

"No." Mark shook his head. "It's bad enough when your sister reacts without thinking through the consequences, but this went too far." He turned to Alyson. "Would it have killed you to wait? To trust your sister a little?"

Alyson didn't say anything.

"All she wanted to do was protect Keera." Scott held out his hand when he saw Mark was about to argue. "Think about it for a moment, please. If it were one of our girls, would we not want to be told, to know that someone wanted to protect our daughters? Sure, she should have waited, and yes, she didn't really think about the ramifications of meeting with Rachel, but calm down, man." Scott's words were all jumbled as he quickly tried to talk Mark down.

"Calm down?" Mark shook his head and then sat down at the table, across from Tricia.

"It was a mistake."

"A mistake?" Mark rubbed his forehead. "Do you have any idea what that mistake is going to cost? Not only us but others? We all know Eddie. We might not like him, but you're"—he looked at Alyson—"accusing him of being a child molester. Can you live with the guilt of what you've done if you're wrong? You're going to destroy his life. You're going to destroy Myah and Keera's life while you're at it."

"What did Rachel say?" Alyson asked quietly.

Tricia waited until everyone, other than her mother, sat down at the table.

"Child Protective Services has to get involved."

Alyson's whole body deflated as she nodded, and Tricia hated to see her sister like that—as if she were carrying the weight of her actions on her shoulders.

"Did you realize that would happen?" Mark asked her. "Did you know, when asking her for coffee, that you were about to open a can of worms no one could ignore?"

"She's not just the principal. She's also a friend." Alyson's chin rose. "That's how I expected her to handle it. I just needed to know if I was overreacting or not and figured she would be the one to know."

Mark laughed.

"Hey, lay off." Scott placed his arm around Alyson. "Alyson's actions weren't wrong."

"How do you know?" Tricia asked. "How do you know that she's right? There's no proof other than what a child said. There is no proof that she has been sexually abused."

"What about what she said though?" Alyson asked.

"What did she say?" Myah asked.

There was a silence in the room as Myah stood in the kitchen, next to Ida, her face stricken from what she'd obviously overheard.

"Myah," Alyson whispered.

"What did Keera say? That's who you're talking about, right? My daughter?"

Tricia rose from the chair and came to stand in front of her friend. "We didn't hear you come in," she said.

"No, but I heard you. From the moment I walked in the door, I heard you." She took a step backward. "I heard you think my daughter is being abused. Is that why Rachel keeps calling me? Is that what she wants to talk about?" Her eyes widened as understanding dawned on her face. "Oh my god, that's why you wanted to talk to me, and asked me about Keera, isn't it?"

"Myah—" Tricia didn't know what to say or even how to say it, but she hated what she saw on her friend's face.

"Let's sit down," Ida said, her voice soft but commanding. She led Myah to the table and stood behind her, her hands on Myah's shoulders. "Everyone needs to calm down and explain to Myah what is going on. Alyson, I suggest you be the one to start."

Alyson took a deep breath and slowly let it out. She fiddled with the napkin on the table, folding and unfolding it, until she raised her gaze, first to Tricia, who came and sat back down, and then to Myah.

"First, let me say that everything I did, it was to protect Keera." She hesitated, as if waiting for Myah to nod, to show she understood, but Myah didn't.

"It's not your responsibility to protect my daughter, Alyson. It's mine," Myah said with quiet determination.

"I know." Alyson nodded. "But I—"

"It's my job," Myah interrupted. "And it's your responsibility as my friend to come and talk to me about any fears you might have."

"You're right, and I'm sorry." There was honesty in Alyson's voice. "Lyla came home yesterday and told me about things that happened at the sleepover, and I got worried. I talked with Tricia who said she would talk with you, but . . ." Alyson's gaze went from Myah to Tricia to her husband, Scott. "But I was worried that everyone thought I was just overreacting once again and wouldn't listen."

"What did Lyla tell you?"

Alyson stared at the table. "When the girls sneaked out to hang with the boys, it was because Keera wanted to see if a boy could kiss like a man, and that—" Her voice broke, and she wiped her face with her palm. "Eddie taught her dances and played games with her as rewards for learning the moves."

Myah gasped.

"I'm sorry, Myah. I should have come to you first. I should have." Alyson reached her hands out toward Myah who only shook her head at her.

"So you think Eddie is . . . that Keera is . . ." Her mouth gaped open as she visibly struggled to find the words.

"I think Keera is being sexually abused by Eddie." Alyson laid it out there, without any hesitation or doubt.

"How? How could you possibly know my daughter is being . . ." She choked. "That Eddie would do . . ." She shook her head in disbelief. "How can you be so sure? Because Lyla told you? Don't you think I would know?" She looked to Tricia then.

Tricia wanted to say something, but Ida shook her head before placing her hands back on Myah's shoulders.

"Sometimes we're the last ones to know," Ida said quietly.

Myah turned in her seat to face Ida. "But I would know. I know the signs . . . I know Eddie."

Tricia couldn't handle it anymore. She pushed her chair back and went to Myah, kneeling on the ground beside her.

"It's not your fault if it's true," she said to her friend, taking her hands and holding them.

"Of course it's my fault. I'm the one who brought him into her life, the one who trusted him . . . but I can't . . . I don't believe . . . he's with her right now at the studio." She leaned forward and pulled her arms in so she wasn't being touched by anyone. "Where is Lyla? I need to hear this myself."

"Myah." Alyson sat up in her seat. "Now isn't the time."

Tricia knew what Alyson was doing, knew that her sister wanted to prepare her daughter, but it was a little too late.

"Aly, she needs to know."

"I've already said what Lyla told me. You don't need to bring her into this. What about Katy? She was there too. Did you talk to her? What did she say?"

Tricia rubbed her wrist and stood. "I talked to Katy. Their stories don't match."

Myah laughed, a loud and vicious laughter that grated the nerves. "You're kidding me." She stood and leaned down, her palms flat on the table. "You've got some nerve, Aly. Before checking facts, you drew your own conclusions and decided to destroy my life." She spread her hands wide. "Welcome to the club. Anyone else want to join in? It's bad enough I have to deal with Eddie's threats about my career, but now you're ruining my name and my family all because of what?" Her arms dropped to her side. "All because you can't deal with your own past? That's not fair, Aly. You can't keep projecting your fears onto others and think it's okay."

"Myah, I think we should check in on Keera and Eddie, like right now."

"No. I don't want to hear anything you have to say. Do me a favor and call Rachel and tell her it's all a mistake?" Her eyes blazed with fury before they changed to fear. "Please? Before it's too late?"

"I . . . I . . ." Alyson tripped over her words.

"It's not all Aly's fault, Myah." Tricia was more than willing to take the blame.

"That's enough." Ida moved back toward the kitchen. "Anger, accusations, and anything else that is happening will not help. Tricia and Alyson will talk with their daughters and get this settled. Myah, we are here to protect you and love you, and I'm sorry we've also hurt you in the process."

"Don't give me the whole 'good intentions' lecture, Ida." Myah gathered her purse in her hands and walked out of the kitchen.

"Myah," Tricia called after her, quickly following and stopping her at the front door. "I'm sorry. I don't know what else to say."

"Tricia, I need to get my daughter. I'll call you later, okay?"

"Why don't I come with you?"

Myah shook her head vehemently. "I've got this. I know my daughter. I know when she's hiding something from me and when something is wrong. I'll find out."

The screen door banged shut behind Myah, and Tricia just stood there, in shock. What just happened?

She turned to find her mother behind her. "I don't know what to do or say or even feel right now," she admitted.

"You're in a difficult position," Ida said. "You want to protect and defend all at the same time. Sometimes life isn't fair. It's how we handle things that matters. And right now, we need to deal with this as a family, figure out what the next steps are and have it dealt with—tonight."

"What did Katy tell you?" Alyson didn't even wait for Tricia to sit back down at the table.

"Alyson, I'm not going to fight or argue with you, okay?"

"Who's fighting?" Alyson said, laying her hand palm up on the table. "I just want to know what Katy said."

"Katy said it was a regular sleepover," Mark answered. "Nothing like you said happened, according to her."

"Do you believe her?" Alyson asked.

"She's our daughter. Of course we're going to believe her. Why would you even ask that?"

"Because it seems like you're asking us to not believe our daughter," Scott spoke up.

"Guys, I appreciate that we all want to stick up for our daughters," said Tricia. "But the issue here isn't a 'she said versus she said' one."

"Of course it is. It's a word game after all. Who's telling the truth? Who's lying? Who's hiding something?" Alyson crossed her arms.

"Exactly," Tricia said. "Something is wrong with this whole picture, don't you think?"

She let her words sink in. Lyla wouldn't say what she'd said without cause. But was it because Keera was actually being molested by Eddie, or was it because Keera was trying to show off? Was Lyla being insecure and telling Alyson what she thought her mother wanted to hear? Was Katy protecting someone by her lies, if she was lying?

"We're all going to be meeting with Rachel and the school tomorrow, not to mention Child Protective Services. I think it would be a good idea to find out the truth tonight, don't you, rather than tomorrow?"

"Mom?"

All heads turned to find Lyla standing there, her eyes wide with fear.

Instantly, Alyson relaxed and pushed her chair back and went to give her daughter a hug. "What is it, hon?"

"What's going on?"

"Nothing." Alyson smoothed her daughter's hair before bending down to give her a kiss on her forehead.

"Principal Burg knows?"

"Yes, honey, she knows. What you told your mom has serious implications," Tricia spoke up. "Can you repeat what you told your mom? I want to make sure I got it right."

"Lyla, go back with your cousins, okay? Let us grown-ups handle this," Scott said to his daughter.

"Lyla, why don't we go and take Opa some more tea, all right?" Ida spoke up and appeared beside her granddaughter with a tea-kettle in hand. "I'm sure he could use a refill." She placed her hand on Lyla's shoulders, directing her back the way she came.

"That was unnecessary," Alyson hissed to Tricia, who returned her look, unfazed.

"No. It was completely necessary. When I asked Katy about the dancing and the game and the real reason why her and Keera sneaked out, do you know what she told me?" Tricia waited until Alyson was back in her seat. "She admitted to the dancing but said the videos and moves were probably too old for Lyla, and then when I mentioned the blindfold, she had no idea what I was talking about." She leaned forward. "Did you hear me, Alyson? She had no idea. Nor about the words Keera supposedly said about Eddie and kissing. None of it. So you see, it was completely necessary. We need to find out the truth of what happened before this goes any further."

Lies, half-truths, secrets . . . They all had a way of becoming larger than life, until they smothered you and everyone around you. Tricia knew this from experience.

She'd be damned if it happened again.

CHAPTER SEVENTEEN

MYAH
SUNDAY AFTERNOON

There were no other cars at the dance studio, other than Eddie's. Which meant he was alone with Keera.

She slammed the car door shut. She inhaled sharply before running toward the front doors and pulling them open, but she was stopped short when they wouldn't budge. Locked? They had a private class booked later today in the back studio, but the front doors shouldn't be locked. They were never locked when they had classes. She pulled again before fumbling for her keys, her hands shaking as she struggled to fit the key into the lock.

She never should have listened to him this morning when he'd called. She should have hung up the phone or better yet, not even answered.

But instead, she'd enjoyed him groveling this morning, begging for some time with Keera to try to fix the misunderstanding between them, and she'd given in. She'd asked her daughter if she wanted to see Eddie and took the gathering of tears to mean yes.

What if those were tears of pain? She'd never forgive herself.

Myah marched ahead and stopped in her tracks when she saw Keera and Eddie up on the stage, dancing to soft music in the background. She recognized the dance right away. He was teaching her the dance that won them the most competitions—the rumba. Their routine had been very sensual, an extension of their love for one another, one of the many components of what made their dance so original and breathtaking.

Also something she'd specifically told Keera she was too young to learn.

They didn't even notice her arrival, not until she turned the music off.

Eddie's hands slowly drifted off of her daughter's body while Keera jumped away as if embarrassed.

"So when were you going to tell me that you wanted to dance competitively?" Myah crossed her arms over her chest and looked at her daughter, unable to even spare a glance at her soon-to-be ex-husband.

"Oh come on, Myah." Eddie chuckled, obviously attempting to break the tension.

"Keera?" She ignored Eddie.

"Eddie says I'm good," Keera mumbled.

"Of course you are, love." Eddie stepped forward.

"You are good, Keera. But you've never shown me any indication or even told me you wanted to do this. If you did, you know I'd support you." Myah stepped toward her daughter. "All you had to do was tell me. Not practice in secret." She placed her hand on her daughter's arm. "Is this why you've been wanting to spend time with Eddie? To dance?" She prayed this was it.

Keera didn't reply.

"Let's go home and talk, okay?" Myah placed her arm around her daughter and held her close. "I love you, Keera," she whispered, before she led her daughter down the stairs and off the dance platform.

"Wait. You're just leaving, like that?" Eddie followed them.

"Go out to the car, okay?" Myah told Keera and then turned to face Eddie. She waited until she heard the door close behind her daughter before she said anything.

"Why lock the doors, Eddie?" Her foot tapped the floor, and she crossed her arms in front of her.

"What?" The confusion on his face was almost laughable and completely unbelievable.

"There are lessons here later today, or did you forget? Not to mention, we have an open-door policy to our members, remember? So why lock the doors?"

"Myah, love, I can tell you're mad. Don't be." Eddie tried to placate her.

"Mad? You think I'm mad, Eddie? I'm bloody furious! If you . . ." She couldn't even say the words.

"If I what?" Eddie stepped forward, closing the distance between them. "Spit it out, love. If I what?"

"If you ever hurt my daughter, I will kill you." The words came out on their own.

For a moment, there was a look in Eddie's eyes, a glimmer of something . . . fear, worry, dread? But it was gone the next instant, causing Myah to wonder if it'd even been there.

"Threatening me now? Myah, that isn't like you. I'd hate for that to come out during our divorce proceedings." His voice was low, gentle almost.

"It's not a threat, Eddie." It was a promise. If he were hurting her daughter, he'd be the one destroyed. She'd make sure of it.

"Keera is very special. We both know it. There's more to her than meets the eye. If you won't mold and shape her to be the woman she can be, then I will." He took another step forward, but rather than take a step back, as she knew he expected, she stepped forward until there was only an inch of space between their bodies.

"You will have *nothing* to do with molding my daughter into the woman she will grow to be. Do you understand that?" She jabbed a finger into his chest. "If you have hurt her in any way, touched her in any way that is inappropriate, I will destroy you. Do you understand me?" She jabbed again and enjoyed the way he winced as her finger dug into his chest.

He backed away, his hands up high in surrender. "I would never hurt Keera. Never. I swear, Myah."

She turned on her heel and marched out of the theater, head held high, while Eddie continued to speak of his innocence, of his love for Keera and Myah.

When she pushed open the door and listened to it slam behind her, she finally let herself relax a bit.

Keera sat in the car, her legs drawn up to her chest, and even though she hated that her shoes were on the seat, Myah didn't say anything as she got in and turned the ignition.

Silence reigned in the car while Myah drove home, this time obeying the speed limits. She was trying to read her daughter, but Keera was closed off, and Myah wasn't sure what to say. So instead she kept quiet and waited until they got home.

"Keera." Myah stopped her daughter as she was poised to head upstairs once they walked in the door. "Honey, can we talk?"

"Do we have to?" Keera mumbled. She wasn't looking at Myah but rather stared downward, as if there was something of interest on the stairs.

"Yes, honey, we have to. Come on, I'll make hot chocolate." Myah walked ahead to the kitchen, trusting that her daughter would follow.

"Since when did we start keeping secrets from each other?"

Keera's head popped up with alarm before she quickly looked down at the floor again.

"Did I miss some spots when I swept earlier?" Myah asked.

"No."

"So why not look at me rather than the floor? I promise to be more entertaining." Myah smiled, hoping to alleviate some of the tension in the room.

Keera shrugged and sat down at the table. "What are we talking about? I'm already grounded, and you've taken my phone away. What's next? I can't watch my shows—do I have to read a book?"

"God forbid you actually read. What about those books I bought for your birthday, have you read them?"

"That's what you want to talk about? Books?" There was a hint of disgust and confusion in her daughter's voice.

Myah poured hot water from the kettle into the waiting mugs and stirred before adding whipped cream. She didn't say anything, just let her daughter sit there wondering, while she tried to think of the right way to bring the subject up.

"Keera," she said as she placed the cups of hot chocolate on the table. "If you wanted to dance competitively, you should have told me."

Keera shrugged. "I still don't know."

"But why would you ask Eddie to train you? You could have asked me."

"He said you wouldn't let me."

Myah frowned. "You and I both know I don't let Eddie speak for me. I didn't want to push you into something you didn't want to do. You know that. But if you want to, then that's a different story."

"Anyway, Keera." Myah tried again, quietly. "Don't you think it's odd that Eddie wants to spend time with you now? He never really showed any interest before."

"He said you would say that."

Myah sat back. "He did, did he?"

Keera nodded. "He told me he realized too late how important I am to him, and that if he wanted to win you back, he had to show you just how much he"—Keera's voice dropped, and she stared down at her hot chocolate—"loved me."

"Honey." Myah hesitated. "My marriage to Eddie is over. I thought you were okay with that."

Keera shrugged. "I didn't say I agreed or even believed him. But he told me that it was because of me you were leaving him."

Myah sighed. "He lied. You know this. Even if I hadn't caught him cheating on me, I would have kicked his . . . butt . . . to the curb."

"Swear if you want, Mom. I can handle it." Keera's chin lifted and her posture straightened. "I hear worse at school, believe me."

Her daughter was growing up a little faster than she would prefer.

"Okay then, let me ask you a grown-up question." She hesitated and sighed. There was no easy way to ask it.

"Has Eddie ever touched you or done anything to you that made you uncomfortable?"

As if struck by lightning, Keera jolted, almost spilling her hot chocolate.

"God, Mom. For real? That's what you wanted to talk about?" Her face scrunched up in disgust. "You're so gross."

Myah's eyebrow rose. This wasn't the reply she'd expected.

"So he hasn't touched you or kissed you . . . ?" She still couldn't believe she was talking to her eleven-year-old about this, or that she could seem so calm about it. Inside, her emotions were all over the place—fear that it was true, disgust toward Eddie, guilt at herself. But mostly fear.

"Why would you ask me that?" Keera's forehead furrowed, but she wouldn't look at Myah.

"Because Lyla told her mom the reason you wanted to sneak out to meet the boys at the sleepover was to see if a boy kissed like a man."

Keera snapped her head up and looked at Myah before she looked downward again. Her cheeks were stained red, and Myah's heart sank.

"Did you say that?" she asked. Inside she was screaming, *Say it's not true. Say it's not true!* But she knew, even if Keera did say it, she wouldn't be able to believe her.

Keera shook her head. "She's lying."

"Lyla?"

Keera nodded.

"Are you sure?" Myah turned and reached out to her daughter, touching her arm. "Honey, if something happened, you can tell me."

Keera sat there, her body trembling beneath Myah's fingers, but she held her ground.

"Of course I'm sure. She's lying. Why would you take her word over mine? She shouldn't even have been there. She's too young." The denial from her daughter and the attitude toward her friend shocked Myah.

"She's the same age as you. And she's your friend. A friend that is worried about you."

"She's just a kid, Mom. I get it, she's my age, but she doesn't act like it. She wouldn't even watch music videos with us. She kept saying her mom wouldn't like it." The look of disgust on Keera's face bothered Myah.

"I hope you would do the same if you knew I wouldn't approve of something your friends wanted you to do. She also told her mom that you wanted to play a game with a blindfold, where you write on each other's skin, and that this was a game Eddie played with you. Is that a lie too?"

Keera nodded, but this time she kept quiet.

Myah sighed. "I need you to be sure. Lyla's mom told the principal, and now we're all going to have a meeting about it tomorrow."

Her daughter's eyes widened with fear. There was no question her daughter was petrified. She hugged her arms close to her chest, and for a moment, Myah thought for sure she was going to cry.

"Why would she do that? Why does she have to ruin everything?" Keera pushed herself back from the table and fled up the stairs, her steps pounding on each step as she ran up.

Myah followed her, not happy with how their conversation had ended. In her heart, she knew something was wrong, but why wouldn't Keera admit it?

CHAPTER EIGHTEEN

TRICIA
SUNDAY NIGHT

It was eleven o'clock at night. Tricia should be home in bed with Mark, but instead she was sitting on Myah's couch.

"I'm sorry I called. You should be in bed sleeping, not having to talk me off a cliff." Myah curled her long and lithe legs beneath her on the couch and draped a throw over herself.

"You honestly think I'd be sleeping?" Tricia snagged a corner of the throw and covered her cold feet. Huge cups of tea sat on the coffee table in front of them, although Tricia was sure a little bit of alcohol had found its way into Myah's mug.

"I don't know what to do Tricia." Myah sighed as she pulled her long hair into a ponytail.

"Myah, I'm so sorry. I wish . . . I wanted to discuss what Lyla had said to Alyson before mentioning it to you. I wanted to know if it was true or not, before I said anything." She wasn't sure how she could explain what happened, what she'd expected, or . . .

"Would you still have told me? Even if it turned out not to be true?" Myah asked.

Tricia nodded. "Of course I would have. This is something that obviously concerns our girls and their relationship. I just wanted to know what went on first."

Myah nodded and reached out for Tricia's hand. "It's okay. I trust you. You know that right?" She gave Tricia a sad smile. "Besides, I think your sister is right."

Tricia paused, not sure if she heard Myah right.

Myah resettled on the couch, fiddling with the blanket until it fully covered her lap. "I know you never liked Eddie, but I thought I saw something in him you didn't. I wish"—her voice broke—"god, how I wished I had listened to you." Tears gathered, and she quickly wiped them away. "I don't want to believe it. I really don't. But it makes sense when you add everything up, right?" Myah's voice, muffled by tears, dropped low.

"You called him a slimeball, but he's so much more than that. He's a monster." Myah broke down, her body hunched over itself while she cried.

Tricia reached over and placed her hand on Myah's knee.

Myah sniffed. "I should have known better. After he moved out, I should have put my foot down about Keera, but I . . ." She threw her hands out, as if trying to find the words but couldn't.

"You wanted to give him another chance?" Tricia offered.

Myah grabbed a tissue, wiped her nose, and laughed. "God no. I was scared of what he would do. I've seen it before." She laid her head back on the couch and stared up at the ceiling. "Eddie . . . he has some influence. I've seen him in action before. He entwines himself so tightly with those who matter that no one can touch him." She inhaled, shuddering as she did so. "He could destroy me if he wanted. And now I feel so guilty."

"I'm so sorry." Her heart felt like it was breaking. She could only imagine what Myah was feeling right now. "I'm so sorry I wasn't there for you, that I didn't see this, that I didn't pay better attention." Her own voice choked up.

A brief hint of a smile appeared on Myah's face. "Don't apologize." She leaned forward. "You've been there for me, more than you know."

"Did you talk with Keera?"

Myah nodded. "Which leads to my confusion. Her body language tells me something is wrong, but she refuses to admit anything. I caught Eddie teaching her steps to a routine we used to use for competitions. Something Keera isn't ready for and certainly not with him as a partner."

"You didn't know about this, then?"

"Are you kidding me? He knew my feelings on her dancing competitively, so he went behind my back and gave her some spiel about spending more time with her to try to get back with me." She rubbed the back of her head.

"Why don't you go to bed? Tomorrow is going to be a long day."

Myah groaned. "I appreciate what your sister did and why she did it . . . But it's too early to do anything, isn't it? I can't even go to the police."

"Why not?"

"Because she says it's not true. I told her about what Lyla said, and she basically called her a liar."

"What do you mean, she won't admit to anything?"

"I've asked, over and over, but she will not accuse Eddie of anything." Myah leaned forward and grabbed another tissue.

"What did Katy say? Did you talk to her again?" There was a small measure of hope in Myah's gaze, and Tricia hated to break it.

"She won't change her story. She says Lyla is exaggerating and had fallen asleep while they were watching the videos." She rubbed the back of her neck. "But she's hiding something. I know it."

"You don't think . . ." Myah's face blanched.

She could only be thinking one thing. "No. She doesn't like Eddie and hasn't spent any time alone with him. I already asked."

"What is she hiding then?"

"I think she's trying to protect Keera by keeping her secret. Eddie probably threatened Keera in some way, said something to make her think she would get in trouble if anyone found out." She looked down. "I think—"

"I hate him. I hate him with every ounce of my being, and if I could kill him, I would. I would, Tricia. So help me . . ." Her body shuddered, but Tricia knew it was with anger. "Why won't she admit it to me? Why won't she tell me the truth? She can't be scared of me. She knows . . . oh god. What am I going to do?"

"You have to tell someone."

"I can't." Myah shook her head and got up from the couch. "Oh god, Tricia. Do you understand what this is going to do to her? I'll get her help, we'll talk to a counselor, but this can't be made public." A wild look set in. "I won't have her live her life as *that girl*. It'll kill her, destroy her . . ."

"You don't have much of a choice. The meeting tomorrow, it's with Rachel, Child Protective Services, and I'm sure the police . . . you remember that, right?"

Myah shook her head. "No. Rachel wants to meet, but nothing was said about the police or Child Protective Services." A slight edge of hysteria bubbled up in Myah's voice. "What are you talking about?" Myah exploded, her hands raised as she started to talk gibberish, or probably Spanish, her voice low enough not to wake Keera, but loud enough to get the point across.

"I love your sister, I really do. But please explain why she wouldn't talk to me first before approaching Rachel?" Myah crossed her arms, her lips tight as she waited for Tricia to answer a question she had no answer to.

So instead, she shrugged. "Why does Aly do half the things she does? Because she panics."

"Not good enough."

"Myah, it all kind of went crazy and snowballed. I hate to admit it, but I didn't believe her at first. It's the time of year, and she always gets . . . paranoid and off-centered around now. So I thought it was her paranoia talking. I wish . . . I wish I had believed her."

"No . . . don't beat yourself up. Don't. But I need to know the whole story."

"Here's the thing. You're not alone now. Same with Keera."

"But she hasn't admitted anything to me, and yet she did to your girls. What's going to happen tomorrow? How is she going to feel?" Myah wrung her hands together.

"Talk to her. Let her know what's going to happen, and let her know she's safe."

"I've got classes in the morning."

Seriously? She was worried about her classes? "Cancel them or find someone to cover for you."

"I'm going to start losing students if I keep doing this. The moms are already complaining. I can't afford it."

An idea percolated within Tricia. "Are you talking about the class Lyla is in?"

Myah nodded.

Perfect. She pulled out her phone. "Then I know the perfect person to take care of this for you."

CHAPTER NINETEEN

ALYSON
EARLY MONDAY MORNING

The early yoga class for the girls was off to a great start. Nearly everyone was here, except for Myah. Settled in her usual spot, Alyson held her coffee in her hand and looked around the studio. Many of the women were frowning. She'd expected the substitute instructor to have shown up by now, and she could tell by the looks on the women around her they were not pleased.

"Seriously?" Melinda Brown took the seat next to her. "Late again? This class was her idea, and she's not even here?" Alyson frowned in annoyance. Why her? Why did this woman always have to pick her to sit beside?

"I swear, if we get another fill-in, I'm pulling Maryanne. I don't care how yoga will help the girls with their dance, or even how expensive her husband is, at least he wouldn't pull this crap. And honestly," Melinda said with a shrug, "I think all this yoga for dance crap is just that: crap."

Alyson thought about the text she'd received late last night from her sister.

Alyson turned toward Melinda and gave her the fakest smile she could manage. "Really, Melinda? Considering his classes are twice as long, not to mention he requires more discipline than I'm sure your daughter can handle, are you really sure about that? Plus"—she knew this part was really snarky, but she didn't care—"he makes parents agree to volunteer activities. You're really going to pull her? And you're going to complain about this class when it was your idea after reading about that program in the city that offers morning yoga to the dancers?" She turned back in her seat. "Besides, from what I hear, he might not be the type of person you want your daughter around." Despite her voice being very low, she knew Melinda heard her.

"Well," Melinda huffed, turning away to gossip with another woman.

She was glad Myah wasn't here.

Lyla came over to where she sat. "My stomach doesn't feel good," she whispered into Alyson's ear.

Alyson gently rubbed her daughter's back. She'd been like this all night and this morning. They probably shouldn't have come, but Scott thought going to dance would help take her mind off things, even if only for a little while.

"Deep breaths, okay, honey? Just relax and try to have fun this morning. If it gets really bad, we can leave. But, let's try to stick it out, okay?" Alyson's voice was low so as not to be overheard.

"Okay."

After dinner, there'd been a talk between the parents and Lyla and Katy, trying to find out the truth of what happened at the sleepover, but other than Lyla crying that she was telling the truth and Katy refusing to say a word, nothing had been accomplished. Tricia and Alyson agreed to talk to their daughters again before they went to school, but this morning when she'd texted Tricia asking if Katy had said anything, her sister replied with only one word. Silence.

"Figures." Melinda shook her head in disgust when Jessie walked in. "I'm going to complain."

Alyson inhaled deeply and let it out slowly. Screw it. She didn't need to remain calm.

"You know, maybe there's something going on with Myah. Have you thought of that? How about instead of condemning a woman for not being here, you find out what is going on first?" She pushed herself up from her seat and reached for Lyla's hand. "For heaven's sake. It's only a yoga class."

"Do you want to get out of here?" she asked her daughter. Lyla stared up at her with wide eyes and nodded. "Go grab your stuff."

Alyson had sent her sister a text this morning letting her know the time of her meeting with Rachel and wondering when Tricia's was, but hadn't gotten a reply. She felt like she was being ostracized, and she didn't like it one bit.

She pulled out her phone to check whether Tricia had responded, and thankfully, there was a message from her.

Everything is going to be okay. Stop stressing. Lyla will be fine.

Is Myah okay? she texted back.

No, but she'll get through. We'll help her, right?

Right. She placed her phone back in her bag.

"Ready?" Lyla had appeared at her side.

Alyson smiled. "Ready. Do you think your stomach can handle a smoothie? We have time to stop before school. And you should eat something."

Lyla nodded and then grabbed hold of Alyson's hand, squeezing tight.

Between now and the meeting at the school, Alyson wanted to remain cheerful.

Scott thought she should tell Lyla about her own experience, that knowing she understood what Lyla must be going through might help. He was right, and yet she couldn't.

She just . . . couldn't.

CHAPTER TWENTY

TRICIA
MONDAY MORNING

Tricia read her sister's text discreetly and responded, hoping no one else noticed.

"Katy, I know this has to be hard for you, but I want to thank you for coming in with your mom so early." Rachel sat next to Katy and Tricia in her office.

Tricia knew she sat there strategically, to help put Katy at ease, but it wasn't working. It didn't help that a member of the school board, Sandra McAdams, stood off to the side, her arms crossed as she listened in on the conversation.

"Why isn't Lyla here too, Mrs. Burg?" Katy asked.

Tricia hadn't been sure how Katy would react this morning. When she'd first told her of the meeting this morning, her daughter had been sullen at first, arguing that she didn't think she should have to go and that she wasn't happy with Aunt Alyson at the moment. But her emotions quickly changed once they were in the car on their way to the school, and it didn't take a genius to know her daughter was nervous.

Tricia had tried to talk to her, but the moment she was in the car, she had her music on and headphones plugged in.

Tricia reached over, wanting to gently touch her daughter's arm, to let her know it was okay, but the way Katy's arm moved, just an inch, before she could, stopped her.

"I wanted to talk with you first, Katy. I hope that's okay." Rachel leaned forward in her seat.

Katy shrugged.

"I know you and Keera are really close friends, right?"

Tricia knew from her phone call with Rachel yesterday that Rachel had to be careful with her questions—Rachel needed Katy to tell her in her own words what happened rather than confirm or agree with anything Rachel asked. She also knew that it was important for a member of the school board to be present—that this was even above Rachel's head.

"She's my best friend." Katy corrected her.

"Sorry, best friends. Can you tell me a little bit about what happened this past weekend during your sleepover?" Rachel smiled at Tricia briefly.

Katy shrugged. Again with the shrugs.

"Katy, use your words please," Tricia said beneath her breath.

"Fine. What parts?" She looked up at Tricia. "Do I need to tell her about . . . you know?"

It bothered Tricia how Katy was reacting. She was about to say something, but a look from Rachel stopped her, so instead, she just nodded.

"If the 'you know' was the sneaking out of the basement part, then yes," Rachel said.

Katy thought about that for a moment and then shook her head.

"How come? We already dealt with it at home. It's not fair that I get in trouble about it again here." Katy gripped her hands together in her lap.

"Katy, we already talked about it. Why are you acting this way?" Tricia asked.

Her daughter shrugged. "Why am I here?"

"Katherine—" Tricia had had enough of her daughter's flippant attitude, but Rachel stopped her by raising her hand.

"That's a good question." Her voice was very patient. "Let me start off by saying, no, you're not in trouble, and I'm sorry for making you feel that way," Rachel said. "Can you tell me more about the videos you all watched?"

"Why? You're not my parent."

"Katherine Edwards." Tricia was shocked at her daughter.

Rachel nodded. "No, you're right. I'm not. But I'm not your enemy either, Katy. You know that."

Katy's gaze lowered. "This sucks."

"I agree," she said. "It does suck. But if you work with me a little bit more, we'll get through this a lot faster."

"We just watched music videos. Then a bunch of us were dancing to them, you know, practicing our moves and stuff."

Rachel glanced over to Sandra who was keeping notes.

"You all did a great job at the recital, by the way. I was really impressed with how well you all did," Rachel said.

Katy blushed. "Thanks. I just started. But Keera rocks. I guess it helps that her parents are both professional dancers."

"Can we talk about those dance moves?"

"Do we have to?" Katy said.

"Is there a reason you'd rather not?" Rachel got up and reached for a bottle of water she had on her desk, taking a drink.

Katy turned to Tricia. "Can we leave now?" There was a plea in her voice that answered all of Tricia's questions about why Katy had been so quiet.

"She asked you not to, didn't she?" Tricia said.

A wide range of emotions flashed across Katy's face.

"You know, trust between friends *is* really important." Rachel broke the tension in the room. "And normally I wouldn't ask you to betray that trust, except, I think you need to, Katy."

"Why?"

"Because in this case, you'll be protecting her, helping to keep her safe, if you do."

"She said we would get in trouble. That you'd be mad at me." Confusion filled her face as she looked to Tricia.

"You should know me better than that, honey." Tricia reached over and squeezed her daughter's hand.

No one said anything until Sandra spoke up. "Can you tell us about the videos you watched?"

"Like what?" Katy breathed a little easier at the change of direction the question took them.

"Did Keera show you any dance moves her father taught her?"

Katy slowly nodded her head.

"Did you try them?"

"It wasn't that big of a deal. It's nothing Keera's mom would teach her, but her dad says she can handle it, that if she wants to get more serious with dancing, then she needs to learn how to dance like an adult, not like a child."

"Fair enough." Rachel obviously wasn't going to challenge the statement even though she obviously disagreed. "What did you do after the dancing?"

Katy thought for a moment. "We made up some stories. It was Lyla's idea. She started, and then we'd go round and make up a story until it was done. They were lame though. So Keera suggested a game of Dare."

The game of Dare was news to Tricia.

"Was that the only game you guys played?"

Katy looked down at her lap.

"Is there something you're not telling me? Something I don't know to ask maybe?" Rachel said quietly.

Katy leaned forward and dropped her head. She mumbled something.

"Could you repeat that?" Rachel asked.

Katy shook her head.

"Remember what I said about needing to keep someone safe and sometimes having to tell their secrets?" Rachel sat on the edge of her chair.

No response from Katy.

"Katy, you're not here to get Keera in trouble. You're here because I think she's getting hurt in a way no girl should ever be hurt, and we want to stop that." Sandra cleared her throat at Rachel's statement, but Rachel ignored her. "She's not in trouble, you're not in trouble, and in fact, you're being the best kind of friend to her right now."

"Katy, it's important. Please?" Tricia asked.

"Keera wanted to play a game, one that she played with . . ." She looked at Tricia, and tears filled her eyes. She quickly wiped them away. "Her dad taught her this game, as a reward for learning those hard dance routines."

"What kind of game?" The tone of Rachel's voice was gentle and almost flat.

"One person was blindfolded. The other two would touch that person's skin with stuff. Like a feather, a pencil . . . whatever we could find around my room. That person had to guess what we were touching them with." Katy shrugged. "It wasn't bad or anything though."

"And the game was a reward from Keera's dad?"

"Yeah. But she told me to not tell anyone. Her dad said people would think things and try to stop him from teaching her the dances, and then she'd never be famous. It's supposed to be a secret and that if I told, I'd get in trouble."

"Well, Katy." Rachel stood up, smoothing her sweater as she did so. "I can promise you that you are definitely not in trouble with me, and I have a feeling your mom feels the same way. I think it took a lot of courage for you to tell me these secrets, so"—she held out her hand for Katy to grab—"thank you."

Katy stood up and slowly reached out for Rachel's hand.

"I do have to ask one more thing, however," Rachel said as they shook hands. "Back to when you and Keera sneaked out of the basement to hang out with the boys, what was the reason for that?"

Katy stuck her hands in the pockets of her jeans. "We just wanted to see what they were doing."

Tricia nudged her daughter.

"Fine. Keera likes Brandon, okay? She wanted to see if he'd kiss her." Her daughter held that defiant look on her face again as she looked up at Tricia and then Rachel.

"Keep going with this attitude, honey, and we'll be having a discussion at home after school," Tricia warned her.

Katy had the decency to look away.

"Katy, every time you give me attitude over a simple question, do you know what it tells me?" Rachel, once again, had a patient look on her face. The woman must do yoga in the mornings to retain this calmness.

"What?"

"That you're keeping something from me." She clasped her hands together in front of her. "Are you?"

"She said she wanted to see if a boy could kiss like a man. But she didn't mean it. She's never been kissed before."

"So why did she say it?" Tricia asked.

"She was just trying to show off, Mom. Some of the other girls were talking about getting kissed by boys, and she didn't want them to know she's never been kissed before."

Tricia's eyebrow rose. "Have you?"

Katy snickered. "As if. Boys are gross." She adjusted her backpack on her shoulder. "Can I go now?"

"Thanks for coming in, Katy," Rachel said. "Do me a favor? Keep this conversation to yourself, especially with your friends in class, okay?"

The look on Katy's face was priceless, and Tricia tried not to laugh. She may be only eleven, but sometimes she had the attitude of a teenager.

"Yeah, yeah. I got it." Rachel obviously caught the meaning behind her daughter's look. "Thanks for coming in." She walked them to the door and opened it.

Once Katy left the office, Tricia didn't quite know what to say as she packed up to go.

"She's not usually like that."

"She was nothing. You should see some of the kids I get in my office. And we've placed her in a sticky situation." Rachel glanced behind her. "That was really hard for her. She's a good friend not only for wanting to keep Keera's secret but also for telling it. You should be proud of her."

"I am. I spoke with Myah last night," she began to say, before glancing inside the office and catching Sandra staring at them.

"I'd better go," Rachel said quietly. "Please, remember what I said yesterday on the phone—everything has to stay confidential. We'll do our best to keep quiet on our end, but this is a very serious matter. We'll try to keep a tight lid on it, but Eddie Mendez is a big name in our town."

Tricia sighed. "I know."

"You'll need to excuse me . . ." Rachel raised her hand to greet someone behind her, and for a moment, Tricia thought it might be her sister, but when she turned, she didn't recognize the woman.

"Thanks for coming so quickly. Please, come in."

Tricia pulled out her phone.

I'm here when you need me, she texted to Myah.

Meet me at Mom's after, she sent to Alyson. They could discuss things over her mom's strudel and coffee. All of this brought back a lot of memories, and it was time to clear the secrets between her and Aly. She rubbed her wrist at the thought.

Years ago, she'd hid a part of her life from her sister, and at the time, it seemed like a good idea, but now . . . after all of this, she wasn't sure.

CHAPTER TWENTY-ONE

IDA

"Thanks for helping with the boys this morning, Mom." Tricia stood at the door, coffees in hand.

"That's what I'm here for." Ida grabbed her coffee from her daughter's hand. "It's starting to get nippy out there. The boys need new hats and gloves."

"We have lots. I just need to dig the totes out of the basement, something I should have done weeks ago, I guess." Tricia unwrapped her scarf and set it and her coat aside before she followed her mom.

Ida knew she was blessed to live so close to her grandchildren, and she never wanted to take that for granted. She only wished Alyson would let her help as often as Tricia did.

"How was the meeting today?"

"Depends on who you ask. Katy was . . . different. She surprised me with how she acted toward Rachel."

"My Katy?"

"Yes, *your* Katy." Tricia rolled her eyes. "She's ten going on thirteen and has the hormones to prove it. I don't remember being like that at her age."

Ida chuckled. "Oh, honey, not only were you like that . . . you were worse. There was a reason why your father took your door off its frame, don't you remember?"

Tricia shuddered. "Then don't be surprised when I start shipping her over here every so often."

"Oh no you don't." She loved her children and grandchildren, but she would not be *that* kind of grandmother. "I didn't do that with you, and you won't do that with her. That's what being a mom is all about."

Tricia sat down at the table and sighed. She looked miserable, and it broke Ida's heart.

"It was hard, Mom. Harder than I expected it to be," Tricia said. "I'm proud of Katy for telling the truth, but I know it was hard for her to break Keera's trust too. I just hope this doesn't hurt their friendship."

Ida reached across and laid her hand over her daughter's wrist, which she noticed was bare. Where was her bracelet?

"It's going to be okay," she said.

Tricia moved her arms, dropping her hands into her lap and sighed. "Is it? Aly has her meeting this morning. And then it's Myah's turn. The police are going to get involved. We all know that." She cleared her throat. "When I was leaving, this woman arrived and came right in to Rachel's office. I think she was from Child Protective Services. It's getting serious."

"Of course it is." Ida nodded. "And Myah and Keera are going to need you now more than ever. So be there. We'll be there for her too."

Tricia sank back in the chair and sighed.

"Why don't you send your sister a message to drop by? There's some strudel left over from last night." She had to hide it from Gordon this morning so he wouldn't eat it all.

"It's a wonder I'm not five-hundred pounds with the way you feed me." Tricia pretended to groan, but Ida knew better. Like father like daughter. Her strudel had always been one of Tricia's favorite dishes. "And I already did." She gave Ida a cheeky smile, and it warmed Ida's heart.

Ida puttered around her kitchen cleaning it up and setting the strudel on a plate. She also grabbed some healthier muffins that she kept in the freezer to defrost for Alyson.

Her gaze kept going to her daughter's bare wrist, and she remembered something she'd picked up as a Christmas gift, but maybe . . . maybe she'd give it to her today.

"I'll be right back," she said as she made her way to her craft room. She moved a few piles of wrapping paper and gift bags and eventually found what she was looking for.

"What are you doing?" Tricia stood there in the doorway. "How can you find anything in this room?"

"I know exactly where everything is. And you shouldn't be in here."

"Why?" Tricia chuckled. "Are you embarrassed to actually have a room that isn't spotless and organized?"

Thankfully, Ida heard the teasing in her daughter's voice.

"*Oh, Scher dich weg,*" she said. Be off with you. "Go on, get." Ida forced her daughter out of the room and back into the kitchen, where she handed her the little gift box.

"What's this?" Tricia hesitated as she glanced at the box.

"Just a little something I found for you, that's all. Nothing special. But,"—she waited as Tricia unwrapped the bracelet from the tissue—"I noticed you weren't wearing your bracelet today, so . . ." She let her voice trail off, not sure how to finish the sentence. Tricia's scar on her wrist was another thing from the past they didn't talk about.

"The clasp broke on me. I think it got caught on something," Tricia said quietly as she gazed at the brown leather cuff bracelet where the words *strength courage love* were etched on a beautiful band. "This is so pretty, Mom. Thank you."

Ida reached out and gave her daughter a hug before she took the bracelet and wrapped it around her wrist. "I thought of you when I saw it." She smiled up at Tricia and knew her love for her daughter filled her very being. "I've never known someone with more strength, more love, and more courage than you. Ever."

Ida patted her daughter's hand and walked back toward the kitchen table.

"Mom," Tricia called out. Ida turned around. "Thank you. For everything. But you know it wasn't your fault, right?"

Ida's hand came up and brushed the air. "It's nothing. A mother likes to buy her daughters gifts, that's all." She didn't like getting overly emotional about these things. And despite what Tricia said, they both knew it was her fault. She should have seen, should have noticed . . . should have protected her daughter better. Ida understood Alyson's deep need to protect her daughter. She understood all too well.

"Wasn't it Oprah who said 'Love is in the details'?"

Ida's gaze tilted upward as if recalling a memory, but then a very small twitch began to show at the corner of her mouth. "Well, it was someone obviously wise. Although, I like to think I was the one who said it first." She struggled to keep the smile off her face, but as Tricia's eyebrow arched, she couldn't help herself.

"Now, tell me what else is bothering you. How can I help?" Ida reached over and placed her hand on one of Tricia's and squeezed.

Tricia weighed her words, knowing her mother wasn't going to like what she was about to say. "We have a lot of secrets in our family."

"Tricia." Ida didn't need her daughter to say anything else. "Some secrets are best left alone. Let it lie. Leave it in the past. Please."

Her daughter shook her head and tears fell from her eyes. "I can't. Not anymore."

"Why? Why now?"

"Because of Keera."

"Keera is a child. You're an adult. There's a big difference." Ida grabbed a dishcloth and began wiping down her counter.

"I was only a few years older than her, and Aly was her age."

Ida scrubbed hard at the imagined stain. She did not want to talk about this. Why did Tricia have to dredge all of this up now? Wasn't it enough that they had to go through this with Myah?

"This is going to be hard enough on your sister. You know how she is at this time of the year. Why bring back painful memories when you don't have to?"

"Don't you think it's hard on me too?" Tricia's voice broke, and Ida buried her head even more. "Mom, look at me. Please."

Ida slowly looked up and saw the desperation on her daughter's face. She dropped her cloth and rushed over, enveloping Tricia in her arms.

"I know it's hard on you. But you've always been stronger." Ida kissed Tricia's forehead.

Tricia held out her wrist and pushed the leather apart until her scar was visible. "I'm not strong, Mom. I just know how to bury my pain."

"No, no. You don't bury. You dealt with it. I know you did. You never needed me. You were always so strong. Reminded me of my own Mutter. So strong." Despite all the hardships growing up, her own mom never cried, never broke down.

Tricia started to laugh while she cried at the same time. "The strong one is Alyson. I realized that last night. She knows who she is. She was the one who noticed Keera, Mom. Alyson did. The one we thought weak. The one we keep trying to protect."

"Then we did a good job." Ida straightened. She didn't understand what Tricia was saying. There was no comparison between the two girls. Alyson always lived in the past, letting it control her.

Tricia didn't say anything, and Ida wasn't sure what she'd said that was so wrong.

CHAPTER TWENTY-TWO

MYAH
LATE MONDAY MORNING

Myah kept her hand on Keera's back as they made their way into the school and to the main office. They sat there, in the most uncomfortable seats imaginable, while they waited for Rachel.

Myah wasn't too familiar with Rachel, despite her being good friends with Alyson.

"I don't want to do this, Mom. I really don't. Please? Can you just tell her that it was all a mistake?"

"I can't, Keera." Myah rubbed her arms to ward off a chill.

This wasn't the first time Keera had asked this of her. It broke her heart to hear the fear in her daughter's voice, but it also made her more determined to make sure her daughter got the help she needed.

"Keera?" Rachel stood there, dressed smartly with her hair pulled into a bun. She smiled. "Myah, thanks for coming in."

Myah nodded and followed Rachel down the hallway and into her office. She held Keera's hand all the way, hoping to offer her daughter some reassurance.

She halted when they came to the open door. She'd assumed it would be just them, the three of them in this meeting.

"Myah, let me introduce Sandra McAdams, our school board trustee. And this is Ms. Jacobs, from Child Protective Services." Rachel clasped her hands tightly in front of her and waited while Myah stood rooted with Keera at her side. "Do you want to come in and sit?"

"Of course." Myah forced a smile on her face as her daughter glanced up with fear in her eyes. "It's going to be okay," she whispered.

"Keera, thank you for coming in. I spoke with your teacher already, so she knows you'll be slightly late to class."

"She knows I'm in here?" Keera's eyes grew wide, and her gaze dropped down to her hands immediately after she spoke. "Does she know why?"

"Don't worry. What you say in here is strictly confidential. All she knows is that we're meeting in here with your mom."

Keera bit her lip. "Okay."

The social worker stepped forward and sat in one of the empty chairs, and then Rachel sat in the other.

"Keera, my name is Debra. I'm from Child Protective Services, and the reason I'm here is because I try to help keep kids safe and make sure no one is hurting them. I know it's not easy being here, and you're probably really scared, but I just have a few questions to ask you, okay?" The social worker sat at the edge of her chair, her hands folded over her knee and smiled.

"Can you tell me a little about your sleepover at Katy's house Friday night?"

Keera's face scrunched up. "Like what?"

Debra uncrossed her legs and smoothed a hand over her knee. "Like things you did, games you played . . . anything like that."

"We watched a movie then some videos, had a dance-off, and then went to sleep. Stuff like that?"

Debra nodded. "Stuff like that is perfect. I was at the dance recital. I thought you were very good."

Keera cocked her head slightly. "You were?"

"I was. I know a few girls who were up there with you. I could tell you've been dancing for a long time, but it probably helps that your mom is a famous dancer too, right?"

Keera nodded. "And Eddie too."

Debra kept her attention solely focused on Keera, but Myah noticed a subtle shift to her posture, almost as if she needed Keera to bring up the subject of Eddie and not the other way around.

Please let this work, Myah prayed. She needed Keera to open up, to admit that something happened.

"That's right. Eddie was your mom's dance partner before they married. So he's been in your life for a long time, hasn't he?"

Keera nodded.

"Have you always gotten along?"

Keera shifted in her seat and frowned. "No. He's not really at the top of my favorite list, you know? I was glad when my mom asked him to leave." She peeked at Myah out of the corner of her eye, and Myah sighed.

"Is this true, Mom?" Debra turned toward Myah, an interested look on her face.

Myah nodded. "It was something Keera and I talked a lot about. Her and Eddie . . . they never really got along, and that's not what I wanted for Keera. So before we separated, I made sure Keera was okay with it."

"And you were?" Debra asked Keera.

Her daughter nodded.

"Do you see much of Eddie now that your mom left him?"

Again, her daughter nodded, but this time her movement was a bit jerkier.

"He's been asking to see her more and more," Myah mentioned.

Debra's lips pursed together. "Is that right, Keera?"

Confused, Myah looked toward Rachel, who only shook her head. Then it clicked—Debra probably needed to hear it from Keera, without any help from her. Myah sighed and sat back in the chair.

"He's been wanting to take me for breakfast and teach me some new dance routines."

"Do you like spending time with him?" Debra asked.

Keera remained silent.

"When he teaches you the new dance moves, are you guys alone?"

"It's okay, honey," Myah said quietly.

Once again, she'd let her daughter down. They shouldn't have been in this situation to begin with—she should have protected Keera more, seen the signs, refused Eddie any access to her the moment he left the house.

Because she knew nothing had happened between them while he'd still lived with them, right? She would have known. Besides, Keera hardly ever stayed at the house alone with Eddie—whenever Myah had a late class or anything, Keera always made arrangements to either go with her to the dance hall or beg to be dropped off at Tricia's house.

Oh god.

How had she not seen it? How could she have been so blind?

"Myah?" Rachel was at her side, squeezing her shoulder. "Myah, are you okay? How about we step out into the hall for a moment, will that be okay?"

Dazed, Myah looked up and caught the look of concern on the faces around her.

"Myah?" Rachel held out her hand for Myah to take.

"I'm sorry, I just"—she had a hard time swallowing—"I just remembered something."

"No worries. We're okay in here if you need a moment."

Myah followed Rachel out into the hallway, wiping at the tears that streamed down her face. She waited for the door to close before she covered her face with her hands and silently sobbed.

Rachel placed her arms around her, holding her tight while Myah cried against her shoulder.

"It's going to be okay," Rachel murmured.

Myah shook her head. "It's not. It's all my fault. I never . . . Oh god, I never saw it. How could I have let it . . ."

Children should always be able to trust their mother to protect them, to shelter them, to keep them from harm. What she'd done was the worst thing possible—she'd brought a monster into her daughter's world.

"What's going to happen now?" she'd tearfully asked Rachel once she managed to regain a little bit of composure.

The look on Rachel's face was hard to see. "Debra needs to make sure something did happen. Once she knows, the police will need to get involved. They'll want to talk to you as well."

Myah sagged against the wall. "I should have seen it. Why didn't I? I was just complaining to Tricia a few days ago that things were off with him. Why didn't I see it?" She shook her head, upset with herself.

"Myah, you can't blame yourself. You can't. Sometimes the person closest is the last one to know. What's important is that we're here, now, trying to give her the help she needs."

Rachel handed Myah a tissue and then went to get her a drink of water. By the time she returned, Myah had calmed herself down.

Now was not the time to fall apart.

As Rachel arrived, she turned toward the door and noticed Debra had stood up and was motioning them to come in.

Myah went immediately to her daughter, who was hunched over, her arms wrapped tight around her body. Debra pulled Rachel to the side and quietly spoke to her.

"Honey, are you okay?" Myah knelt down on the floor and gently wiped the tears that flowed down Keera's face. "It's going to be okay, I promise. It's going to be okay."

CHAPTER TWENTY-THREE

ALYSON

From the moment she stepped into her mother's house, Alyson knew she'd interrupted something. Her mother's smile was bright but pinched, and Tricia didn't even bother to hide her lack of enthusiasm.

"She was okay?" Tricia asked her.

Alyson stared at her sister from across the table and considered her words carefully. In the ten minutes she'd been at her mother's house, she'd thought long and hard about what she would tell her family about the meeting at the school.

"Alyson?" Tricia asked again.

"She amazed me. All I've ever wanted to do was protect her from stuff like this. And yet, when she realized how her side of the story could help Keera, she found her inner strength and told Rachel exactly what had happened. I was so proud of her."

"She gets her strength from you." Tricia finally smiled, and Alyson couldn't help but smile back.

What there was to smile about in this situation, she wasn't sure, but smile she would. Out of everything that could have happened today, her daughter being so strong was not something she'd expected. Her daughter was growing up.

"The one thing she was worried about the most though, was breaking her promise to Keera. Did Katy say anything about that?"

Tricia's smile disappeared.

"I think that was the only thing Katy was worried about," she said quietly. "If Rachel hadn't convinced her, I'm not sure Katy would have said anything."

Alyson kept quiet.

"What are you thinking?" Tricia prodded.

Alyson twisted the wedding ring on her finger. "I can't stop thinking about Myah and Keera. How is Myah holding up?" She stared into her sister's eyes. "Is she mad at me?" She swallowed hard, nervous about the answer.

"Mad at you? Heavens no." Tricia sat up straighter. "I didn't tell you, did I?"

"Myah thinks it might be true." Tricia stood up and gripped the top edge of her seat.

"She suspected?" Alyson leaned back in her chair, her hands gripped around her coffee cup.

Tricia groaned. "No. Well, a little. She was starting to see the signs but hadn't put it together until yesterday."

"What kind of signs?" Alyson's hand shook.

"The amount of interest Eddie showed in Keera lately, the small gifts, and then the threats."

"He threatened her? With what?"

"He was going to ruin her name and career if she tried to keep Keera from him."

Ida stood up and marched out of the room at Tricia's news. Alyson watched her mother walk away and shook her head with disgust. Go figure. Once again, her mother runs away when things hit too close to home.

"I should have seen it. You did. Why didn't I?"

"I've been through it though, Tricia. I knew what to look for. Don't beat yourself up over it."

"You don't think I know something about this? You don't think I know what it's like to be abused? To be made to feel dirty and worthless and second-class? To have your innocence ripped from you, your heart destroyed, your body mutilated?" Agony laced Tricia's words as she paced in front of Alyson.

"Tricia?" Alyson didn't know what to say. She didn't understand where this was coming from or what to do about it. One moment they were talking about Keera, but the next . . . the next it was as if they were talking about Tricia.

It didn't make sense.

Slowly Tricia unclasped the bracelet she wore and then held her wrist out for Alyson to see.

"Did you never wonder why I always wear these big cuffs? Why you never see my wrist bare? Ever?"

Alyson looked at the scar on her sister's skin in horror. The puckered skin held a pale pink tinge to it, but no one would be able to mistake why it was there.

"You never noticed, did you? Of course not. We kept it a secret from you, just like we kept a lot of things a secret from you. I always wondered if maybe you knew . . ." Tricia finally sat down, her shoulders slumped, her head down.

"I never knew." Alyson wanted to cry—she should cry, but she felt numb inside.

"Of course you didn't."

Alyson heard the resignation. "Why wouldn't I?" And then her sister's words hit her. "What do you mean secrets? What secrets have you kept from me?" She looked around for her mother.

"Think about it, Alyson." Tricia traced the scar on her wrist with her finger.

"You tried to kill yourself." She was stating the obvious, but she couldn't really take in what she was seeing.

"Yes. I tried. And then chickened out, but I cut myself deep enough that I needed stitches." She traced the jagged edges. "But I didn't go to the doctor. Mom stitched me up."

"Of course Mom stitched you up—because that's logical. Why didn't you go to the hospital?" Because that would be the logical thing to do.

"Why didn't you?"

That was a touchy subject, and one Alyson held against her mother.

"Mom," they both said in unison.

"I still don't understand though. When did this happen?" Alyson was racking her brain trying to remember a time when Tricia had been anything but strong.

"First year of college. The stress of everything became too much. Too many secrets, too many assignments, just . . . too much."

"What did I miss? What happened? Why all the secrets?" This was all becoming too much. First, they were discussing the girls, then Myah, and now something was wrong with Tricia.

"Do you think now is the right time?" Ida returned to the kitchen, her arms bearing tea towels and dishcloths she'd obviously just washed. "Shouldn't we be focusing on Myah right now?"

"There's never going to be a right time for you, Mother. *Keine geheimnisse mehr.*" No more secrets.

"Would someone please explain to me what I'm missing? Please."

"You're the reason she kept her attempted suicide a secret from me, aren't you? Just like you wanted to keep my rape a secret too. I should have known." Alyson couldn't hide the disgust she felt, the years of holding it in, pushing it down, and not acknowledging her hurt and pain.

"Let me guess. You didn't want to sully our name even further did you? You thought it might hurt Dad's business, or make you look bad." She sneered.

"That's enough. You don't talk to me like that."

"Why not? If I do, maybe you'll actually let down that wall you hold so dear and actually be honest with me. Do you think?" She turned to her sister, looking for Tricia to agree with her.

"No, I don't. This isn't Mom's fault. Just like it wasn't yours or mine. There's no blame here, Aly."

Taken back, Alyson grabbed her purse. "Really? Because when I look back on my life, do you know what I remember most? Not the pain from the monster who raped me, but the shame. The shame that I experienced from the one person who was supposed to love me the most."

She pushed past Tricia, with the goal of leaving, but Ida stopped her.

"Let me go," Alyson said to her mother.

"No. You'll go back and sit down. You want the truth, then fine. You'll get it. But on my terms, not yours."

"Aly, sit. Please," Tricia begged.

Alyson sat. She placed her purse in front of her on the table and clasped her hands together in her lap. Tension coiled in her belly, and her mouth went dry.

No one spoke.

Ida sighed and then stood. "Might as well make coffee. I have a feeling we'll be here for a while."

"Don't you think you've had enough?" Alyson glanced around at the coffee mugs on the table.

Tricia passed her mug across the table. "Better make it a full pot."

"Baileys?" Ida asked.

"Thanks, Mom."

"Why don't I make it?" Alyson offered. She took the mugs from her mother's hands.

Once the coffee was made, Alyson reached for Tricia's hand and gently touched the scar on her wrist.

"Tell me what happened," she said.

"I don't even know where to begin," Tricia said. "You won't understand this without knowing the beginning—"

"So start there."

Tricia fiddled with the lid to the Baileys bottle, her lips opening and closing as she obviously struggled to find the words.

"Oh for Pete's sake. Give it here." Ida reached for the bottle and with a twist unscrewed the lid Tricia had struggled to open. She poured a generous amount of the creamy substance into her coffee cup before doing the same for Tricia and Alyson.

"I don't remember the pain of cutting my wrist, but I sure do remember the pain of having it stitched back up," she said.

"I tried to freeze it first," Ida mumbled. "With ice cubes. But I did the best I could."

Tricia nodded. "You did. That's all you've ever done—the best you could. But sometimes, the best we can do isn't always enough. If we had gone to the hospital, I'm sure the scar wouldn't be this bad, and maybe I wouldn't have had to hide it all these years," she mused. "But then, if we had gone to the hospital, I would have been kicked out of college, admitted to some kind of rehab, and things would have been so different."

"I didn't want that for you." Ida reached across and touched Tricia's wrist. "I'm sorry if my best wasn't good enough, but it was all I had."

"Maybe that was the problem." Tricia sniffed, and it was then Alyson noticed the sheen of tears in her sister's eyes. "I should have asked for more. What happened to me was just as bad as what happened to Aly, and yet my pain, my anger, my experience . . . it was all ignored."

"Why?" Alyson asked.

Tricia looked her in the eyes. "Because of you. Everything has been because of you."

CHAPTER TWENTY-FOUR

TRICIA

Tricia noticed the look of confusion on Alyson's face and gave a small laugh.

"Haven't you ever realized that everything we've done as a family has been centered around you?"

Alyson shook her head. "It hasn't. I don't know what you're talking about."

Tricia knew Alyson didn't see it, and she got that, she really did, but it just added to the layers of hurt Tricia was feeling right now.

Her phone buzzed, and she quickly glanced down. Unless it was life or death, or Myah, she was going to ignore it. She needed to tell Alyson the truth, all of it, and make her understand.

It was her husband.

I'm thinking of you today.

She smiled. That was exactly what she needed. She'd talked with Mark early this morning about this, and he'd agreed it was time. Time to sweep away all the cobwebs from the past.

Love you. She texted him back.

"Was that Myah?" her mother asked. Tricia shook her head. She was anxious to hear from Myah as well, but she had a feeling her meeting at the school was going to take longer than what Tricia and Alyson experienced.

"You weren't the only person that boy Michael Jacobs hurt, Aly." Tricia cleared her throat.

"Don't say his name." Alyson visibly shuddered.

"It's just a name. Has no power over you unless you let it." Tricia repeated a phrase Ida had said all throughout their childhood.

"Who else did he hurt?"

Tricia looked deep into her sister's eyes, wishing, praying even, that she could see the answer for herself.

Alyson glanced down at Tricia's now turned wrist and visibly retched. She covered her mouth with her palm and shook her head.

"No, no," she whispered.

"Yes," Tricia confirmed. She hated to see the look of horror in her sister's eyes, on her face, as the realization that she hadn't been the only one to be hurt by the boy next door, something she'd always thought was the case.

"Why didn't you tell me? Why?"

At her question, Tricia glanced over at her mother.

This was the question Tricia dreaded having to answer. It had been hard enough telling Mark the truth and seeing the pity and sadness in his eyes. But she wasn't sure if she could handle telling her sister the truth.

"I know that day is hazy for you, that there are parts of it you don't remember fully."

"And yet there are parts that are clear as anything else in my life," Alyson murmured.

"Dad was in Germany on a business trip, and Mom was out somewhere. I can never remember where, never have." Tricia gazed off into the distance. "But I was to keep watch over you. Kenny came over and wanted to play with you."

"I don't remember that," Alyson said.

"Are you sure? You went over to his house and played with him. I watched you play in the yard with him until Michael came out and talked to you. He offered you a soda or something. Do you remember that?"

Alyson inhaled deeply, her body shuddering from the impact. "No. I remember . . . I remember the sound of the screen door hitting the frame and the loud drone of their air conditioner."

"I waited, waited for you to come back out. God"—Tricia released the breath she'd been holding in—"you were in there forever, and I started to get nervous. So I went over. Kenny told me you were helping Michael get snacks for the two of you, but when I knocked on the door, there was no answer. I stepped into the kitchen, and you weren't there either. I called for you, and I thought I heard you call my name, so I walked through the house."

She'd only told this story twice in her life. To her mother and to her husband. She never thought telling her sister would be so difficult or hurt so much.

"I can still remember the sound of your voice as you called my name. I've never heard it again, not from my own kids, and I thank God for that every day." Tremors took over her body, and she hugged her arms close. "I ran up the stairs and heard Michael telling you to shut up. All the doors were open but one, and when I opened it . . ." She had to stop.

The memory of seeing him over her sister—her body visibly ached.

"When I came in, he . . . you got free." Tricia blinked, wiping away the memories and managed a semblance of a smile. "I told you to run, to run home and call someone. The police, our neighbors,

Mom . . . it didn't matter. And run you did. I was so proud of you. I went to follow you, but Michael blocked the way, and he wouldn't let me go." She swallowed then wrapped her hands around her cup of coffee and brought it to her lips, her hands still shaking as she did so.

"Please tell me he didn't . . ." Alyson couldn't get the words out, so Tricia did it for her.

"He did. He promised he would leave you alone if I stayed."

"Ich liebe dich, mein starkes Mädchen." I love you, my strong girl. "You don't have to say more," Ida whispered.

"I do. She needs to know." Tricia couldn't keep it a secret anymore. She couldn't.

"Oh my god, there's more?"

"When I finally made it back to the house, you were hiding in your closet. I had to coax you out, and then I helped you get into the shower. You were in shock, could hardly move, so I stepped in with you and just held you close. When Mom finally came home, we were both huddled in your bed, I was holding you close, and you just sobbed. You couldn't stop."

"I remember that. I remember you holding me, telling me everything was going to be okay, that no one was ever going to hurt me again, that you took care of it." She stared at the table before lifting her gaze. "I thought that meant you took care of it with Michael, that you made sure he would never hurt me again, but . . . that's not what you meant, was it?"

"I did take care of it. He promised me he would never touch you again."

"You let him rape you to protect me."

The moment she said the words, it was as if a damn broke inside of Tricia and the tears ran down her cheeks. She couldn't say anything.

"She did," Ida confirmed. "And you never realized. Not because you were blind to it, but because you couldn't know. You were too fragile. You wouldn't leave your bed, you wouldn't let anyone touch you . . . other than your sister. She was the only one who could comfort you, the only one you would let near you."

"I've always . . . I've always felt safe with you." Alyson reached out to Tricia. "Always."

Tricia took hold of her hand and squeezed. "I know. You were so broken though, that I didn't . . . I couldn't tell you what had happened to me. And then it just became easier not to. It took you a long time to deal with what happened, you couldn't even go back to school for a while, and we worried that if we did tell you, you would spiral back into your shell."

"But that was my decision, not your sister's," Ida clarified.

"So you decided to hide things then?" Alyson asked her. "Just like it was your decision to not deal with what had happened to me? To not go to the authorities? To make me face Mrs. Jacobs and have her call me a liar? It was your decision to pretend that what happened to me and to Tricia didn't?"

Ida shook her head in denial. "No. You remember it wrong. I went to confront the Jacobses, and you followed me. You—"

"I did not," Alyson denied. "You forced me to go over there, to tell them what happened to me. You allowed me to be shamed into believing I was lying."

"No. That's not what happened. I know you believe it is, but it's not. You followed me. You stood just outside their screen door and listened in to our argument. I went over to make that foul woman understand what had happened and to warn her that I was going to the police. And that's when she threatened me. She threatened to destroy your father's company, to besmirch our name publicly, to make you look like a fool and a lovesick child. And I believed her."

Ida leaned her head back in her chair and stared up at the ceiling. "I wish I hadn't. But your father wasn't there, and all I could think about was protecting you girls. That's all that mattered. So I gave in. I didn't report what happened, and to her, it seemed like I ran with my tail tucked between my legs."

"Not just to her," Alyson mumbled.

Tricia just sat there. She wanted to stand up for her mother but didn't. It was time everything came out in the open, all the misunderstandings and lies, the secrets—they all needed to be exposed. So she sat there and watched as Ida struggled to explain things as she should have done years ago.

"Think what you want. You always have. But before you judge me, why not listen to my side of the story first? Yes, I'll admit, I cowered, and I've always been ashamed of that. But I made sure I got revenge, my way. I sold our home, and we moved across town. Not because I was ashamed of you—to keep you away from that family, from that boy. I made sure all our neighbors knew they weren't to be trusted, I had that boy fired from his job, cast enough doubt about Mrs. Jacobs in our town that she soon wasn't welcomed anywhere. Her husband owned a used car lot in town . . . all it took was a few whispered words here and there, and they soon went out of business. We may not have been wealthy, we may not have lived the good life like they did, but your father's name meant a lot in our town . . . enough to do damage, and I used it to my advantage." Ida's chin rose as she told them all she'd done.

"You protected us in your own way," Tricia said.

Ida nodded. "Rape, sexual abuse . . . things were different back then. I did what I could with what I had. I'm sorry you felt I ignored your pain, but I didn't. I protected you as I knew best."

"But what about Tricia?" Alyson asked.

"My job was to protect you, and you needed me," Tricia told her. "I was your big sister. I was the one you'd call for in the middle of the night when you had nightmares, until eventually you just started sleeping with me. Even though I never told you or anyone else what happened to me, helping you, being there for you . . . that was what got me through. I didn't ignore what happened to me, I just . . ." She sought the right words. "I just set it aside. I didn't let it break me. I focused all my pain into making sure you were whole." Then she sighed. "And then I went to college, and I broke."

Alyson touched her scar. "This was you breaking?"

Tricia nodded. "It was like you were my security blanket, what held me together and without you there, without you needing me . . . I had to face what happened to me. I went out on a date, and the guy went too far. I remember coming home that night, but there was no one home."

"We were out at a friend's house and stayed longer than planned. If I had known . . ." Ida clamped her lips shut again as if trying to contain her feelings.

"When you all finally did come home, Mom found me in her bathroom. I'd cut my wrist but didn't go deep enough. I couldn't. So I sat there, huddled in the bathtub with my wrist wrapped in a towel."

"Where was I?" Alyson asked. "Why don't I remember any of this?"

"You were sound asleep. It was too late to go to the hospital, so I stitched Tricia up myself. I had enough brothers falling and cutting themselves when I was younger that I knew what I was doing." Ida glanced over at Tricia's wrist. "Somewhat."

"And that's why . . . that's why you always buy her bracelets? To help her cover the scar. I can't believe . . ." Her voice trailed off. "I can't believe you all kept this from me for so long. I'm not that weak child anymore. I know you think otherwise, but my past doesn't dominate my present or dictate my future. I'm who I am because I made it through. I feel like a fool." Alyson stood up. "Thank you." She leaned over and gave Tricia a long hug. "Thank you for finally telling me, but this is a lot to take in, and frankly, I'm so confused right now. I need some time to really take it all in."

Tricia stood up and hugged her sister back. "I love you, you know." She whispered into her ear, "I'm here when you're ready."

Alyson leaned back and looked Tricia in the eye. Tricia was happy to see a smile on her face. "I know," Alyson said. "I've always known you were there for me. I just wish . . . I always felt lesser, you know? Like there was more I could have done for you, more I should have done. I wish you had told me."

CHAPTER TWENTY-FIVE

MYAH
MONDAY AFTERNOON

With her jacket zipped up to her chin, Myah leaned back against her car in the driveway and stared up into the dark night sky. The stars were covered with clouds, and she had a feeling her life for the next days, weeks, months, even years, would never be the same—the future clouded thanks to mistakes she'd made.

She pulled out a cigarette from her pocket, put it between her lips, and let the weight of it hang while she searched for the lighter.

Before going home, Myah had stopped at the store down the street for milk and picked up a pack of cigarettes, something she hadn't done in years.

But right now, she could use a smoke.

She glanced up at her darkened bedroom window, where her daughter slept in her bed. She'd fallen asleep crying, with Myah holding her, and it broke her heart all over again to listen to her daughter sob in her sleep.

Debra, the Child Protective Services worker, told Keera that today was the beginning of a journey for her, one that involved healing and finding strength she never knew she had. But for Myah, it was the beginning of a nightmare.

The moment her daughter admitted that Eddie sexually abused her, everything changed.

Her hands shook as she held the lighter to her face. The red flare of the cigarette as it burned mesmerized her, and when she inhaled, everything stopped, just for a moment.

She would never forgive herself for bringing that bastard into her daughter's life.

The phone in her pocket buzzed, and she was tempted to ignore it, but she pulled it out and saw Tricia's number pop up. Again.

She should answer. Her friend had been calling all day.

"Hi." Myah dropped the cigarette and ground it under her foot.

"Are you okay?" Tricia asked.

Myah sniffed and wiped her face.

"You're not. Do you need me to come over? I can come right now." The urgency in Tricia's voice had Myah panicking.

"No." She couldn't handle having one more person in front of her, looking at her with a mixture of pity and condemnation.

"But thank you," she added, realizing she came off a bit harsh. "I just . . ."

"You need space," Tricia finished for her.

"I do." Funny how well her friend understood.

"Do you want to talk about it?"

Myah sighed and yawned at the same time.

"Or maybe you need to go to bed," Tricia said. "You're probably exhausted, and I can only imagine—"

"I'm beyond exhausted, Tricia. I'm numb."

"No doubt. But I think that's okay, you know?"

"I hate him, Tricia. I need him to suffer, to be destroyed like he's destroyed my daughter." The words forced themselves out of her raw throat.

"He will."

"The stuff he did to her, made her do to him . . ." She couldn't continue. She couldn't.

"I'll kill him for you."

Myah smiled weakly. "I love you. That was the best thing you could have said."

After a moment of silence, Tricia asked, "Where's Keera now?"

Myah glanced up toward her windows again. "In my bed, finally asleep." She hoped she could sleep through the night. She'd given her daughter a sleepy-time tea along with some aspirin to help with the headache she could see in her daughter's eyes.

"Tomorrow . . . it's not going to be easy," Myah admitted.

"How so?"

She thought back to today. "There was no time to breathe today, not once since we stepped into Rachel's office. But tomorrow, it'll all sink in, and we'll have to figure out how to move forward."

"These next few days, weeks, hell even months, are going to rough, Myah. So just take it day by day and look for the good if you can. One day soon, you'll feel like you can breathe again. But you know you're not alone, right?"

Myah nodded. "Debra said the same thing, that we're not alone."

"How was Debra?"

"Nice. Level headed. Keera seems to like her. She warmed up to her quickly. Thanks to Katy and Lyla, by the time we arrived, the police were on standby. It was hard. Hard to not be able to step in and help Keera, but she needed to say what happened to her in her own words. And she finally did. I wasn't sure . . . but she even admitted to asking Katy and Lyla not to say anything. She was worried they would get in trouble."

"Trouble?"

"Eddie threatened Keera that she would get in trouble if she ever said anything. How could I have married him, Tricia? Why was I so blind . . . ?" She shook her head before glancing at her watch. "Eddie should be in police custody by now." The moment she said those words, she felt the tightness in her chest lessen.

"That was fast." Tricia sounded shocked.

"I mentioned that Eddie has been trying to see Keera behind my back, calling her, sending her text messages." Myah blinked past the tears that quickly pooled in her eyes. "He sent her a private message today through an app I didn't know she had. He sends her photos of himself, Tricia . . ."

"I hope he rots in hell."

"Check Katy's phone please. Make sure you know what every app is and who her friends are. Look at her photos and messages . . . I wish I had. I would have been able to stop this sooner." The regret she'd been trying so hard to squash filled her once again.

"It's over now," Tricia said quietly.

Myah stared down at the ground. "Which part? Him abusing her? Yes. But so much more is just beginning. The doctor's appointments, the counseling sessions, the healing process . . . I don't want my girl to lose her smile, the warm heart that she has, and I'm afraid she will. I'm afraid of what this will have done to her, how it will destroy her, change her life." Myah pinched the bridge of her nose.

"Rachel mentioned to Aly that there might be more kids he's done this to, that they would need to look into his clients."

"Thank God he only taught adult classes, but yes, I pray there's no one else. I want to say I'm sorry for what your girls will go through, but I can't."

"You shouldn't. The girls know and realize how important this is. And even more so, Alyson and I understand." Her friend hesitated a moment. "My mom too," she said.

"Because of Aly's experience, right?"

"Not just Aly."

Myah stood there in shock as Tricia told her about the past she'd kept hidden for so long. She couldn't believe what she was hearing, but she wasn't too surprised either.

"My past isn't who I am today. That's why I never brought it up."

"You don't need to explain," Myah told her, and it was true. "How did your mother handle everything? I've always thought of Ida as a strong German woman, but I never expected . . ." Myah pushed herself away from her car and headed back inside. She slipped off her shoes and curled up on the couch in front of the fireplace.

"You should talk to her."

Myah nodded. "I will. Ida invited us for Thanksgiving dinner. Did you know? She considers us family and says, in her heart, she has three daughters."

"That's my mom. You're coming right?"

"I'm in charge of . . . pickles?"

Tricia laughed. "It's about time. Alyson usually brings those, and she brings these awful organic ones that taste like vinegar. No one touches them other than Aly and Lyla. Scott won't even go near them apparently."

"So they're pretty important then. Good to know. Listen." Myah pulled her legs up to her chest. "I want—no, I need—to say thank you. Thank you for being there for me through all of this, and for being there for me in the upcoming months. Thanks for being my friend and the sister of my heart. Otherwise I'd be all alone, and I would go crazy."

Tricia laughed softly. "Nah, you'd just go hard-core into your dance. I know you." She paused. "I'm always here. Always. And Keera will be okay. She's a good girl, and she has an amazing mother who will always be by her side. Plus," she said as her tone lightened, "you're now an official member of the Wilhem family. You'll never be alone again—whether you want to be or not."

"Right now, I'll take all the family I can get."

"So what's happening tomorrow?" Tricia hated to bring it up.

"A massive upheaval. There might be more interviews, and there's a doctor's appointment. I have a meeting with the lawyer, and then somehow I need to do a dance class after school."

"Can't you cancel?"

Myah frowned. "No. I need to show Keera that nothing has changed, nothing fundamental, at least. This is my job, and where I make my money. Now, I'm not sure if Keera will want to be there, and I'll leave that up to her, but I'll start losing students if I keep getting someone to cover for me."

"Somehow, I doubt you'll lose students, and she can always come to my place, you know that, right."

"Thank you."

"You're not going to lose students though. I wish you would stop worrying about it."

"You never know. People are very judgmental. If I can't protect my own daughter, what's to say I won't let something bad happen to theirs? When it comes to protecting your child, people will do anything they feel is in their best interests. You know that."

CHAPTER TWENTY-SIX

ALYSON
TUESDAY AFTERNOON

The moment she stepped into the large room with Lyla after school, she knew something was wrong. There'd been a low murmur one moment and the next—silence.

A quick look around the room told her that Myah hadn't yet arrived.

Lyla headed over to the other girls in the class, where they all sat on a mat and stretched, and Alyson took her usual seat, in the front, to watch her.

"Is it true?"

Alyson forced a smile on her face, not surprised that it was Melinda who had approached her.

"Is what true?"

Confusion flitted across Melinda's face. "Well, you know. About Myah and Eddie."

Alyson's fake smile slowly melted away, and she arched her eyebrow, but didn't say anything.

"I heard that Eddie was arrested last night on charges of child sexual abuse. Is that true?" Melinda leaned in and mock-whispered.

"Where did you hear that?"

Myah and Alyson had already discussed a plan of attack if something like this happened.

"My sister is on the administrative team at the police station. Is it true? I need to know. My sister has him teaching her daughter private dance lessons." Melinda swallowed visibly.

"You should recommend Myah to her. Especially after hearing something like that. I know I wouldn't want someone with that reputation to give my daughter private lessons."

All Myah had asked Alyson to do was neither confirm nor deny, but to build up Myah if needed. It had been Alyson's decision to not only build up Myah but to tear down slimeball Eddie Mendez as a dance instructor. She would take a lesson from her mother's book and use her words and reputation to her advantage.

"Do you think Myah has any openings?" Another woman who sat behind them leaned forward and tapped Alyson on the shoulder.

Aly turned. "I don't know, but if I were you, I'd ask sooner rather than later. If what Melinda says is true"—and here was the other part of her plan, put the wording back on the gossiper and let her believe she had a role to play in protecting their daughters—"then word will get around."

Her eyes widened in shock.

"I'll tell my sister right away." Melinda pulled out her phone. Alyson looked around. She wasn't the only woman who had her phone out and was typing furiously on the screen.

Myah might not like her actions, but Alyson was pleased.

No child deserved to be hurt the way he'd hurt Keera.

The moment Myah walked into the room without her daughter by her side, she was surrounded by the women in the room wanting

to ensure they could get their daughters in for private lessons, and it
thrilled her heart to see it.

CHAPTER TWENTY-SEVEN

IDA
THANKSGIVING

Ida always enjoyed the American tradition of setting aside a day to give thanks. She had a lot to be thankful for and never forgot that.

Gordon on the other hand could care less about the significance of the day other than food and football.

"Would you help me, you old fool," she called out to him as she struggled to get the leaf for the dining room table out from beneath their stairwell.

"I'm coming. I'm coming," he called as his feet shuffled down the hallway.

Together they pulled it out of the cubbyhole and worked together to get the table extended the way Ida wanted it.

"Why did you have to invite so many people anyways?" he grumbled.

"They are our family. That's enough out of you." She swatted him on the arm and then pushed him back toward the rec room, where she could hear the sounds of a football game playing on the television.

She expected the girls to arrive within the hour, and she wanted the tablecloth at least to be out and ironed. She was in the laundry room ironing when she heard the cascade of running footsteps slap against the floor and the voices of her grandchildren calling out for her. That feeling of thankfulness filled her heart as she smoothed out the last remaining wrinkles and met her daughters in the kitchen.

It had been a few weeks since she'd seen her two daughters together. Alyson had taken Tricia's news of their past pretty hard, and instead of focusing on rebuilding their relationship, she'd focused on helping Myah and Keera, offering to watch Keera after Myah's work schedule got busier.

Last week she'd asked to meet with both Ida and Tricia for a chat. Apparently, Alyson had started to see a counselor.

"Just in time to help set the table." Ida carried in the tablecloth and carefully laid it over the table, flattening out the creases and making sure the cloth lay even on each side.

The girls pulled out the china from the cabinet in the other room, china that Ida had started collecting when she was a newly married woman.

"Smells delicious, Oma." Lyla helped to set the silverware, a huge smile on her face as she sniffed the air.

"We've got turkey, stuffing, potatoes, and casseroles. I expect you to eat your fill, do you hear?" Ida attempted a stern face but quickly lost it as Lyla launched herself into her arms.

"Is there pie too?" her granddaughter whispered excitedly.

"Is there pie, she asks." Ida tsked before she gave Lyla a wink.

Alyson opened up a bag full of dishes she'd brought, and Ida swallowed a groan. "What's that you've got in there?" she asked instead.

"I know you said not to bring anything but juice, but I wanted to try some new vegetable casseroles. Is there room in the oven to keep them warm?" Without waiting for an answer, she pulled open the oven door and slid her dishes onto the bottom rack.

Ida smothered her laughter with a cough.

"Are you getting a cold, Mom?" Alyson asked.

"No, no, just a tickle in my throat."

"Myah is just behind us." Tricia handed cups to Katy.

Ida busied herself in the kitchen with the last-minute preparations while her family around her pitched in to help. In no time, the table was set, and they just waited on Myah.

"She was just behind us." Tricia checked her phone and then set it down. "Has she contacted you, Aly?"

Alyson checked her own phone and shook her head just as the doorbell rang.

While the girls went to answer the door, Gordon came into the kitchen with Mark and Scott. "Is it time to eat yet?" He leaned over and kissed Ida on the check. "Smells good."

"Sorry I'm late." Myah walked in with a bag in hand and set it down on the counter. "Pickles, as promised. Along with some whipping cream for pies." She held on to Keera's hand, who hid behind her mother.

Ida watched Keera, concerned about what she was seeing. Everything was still so new. It had only been a few weeks since her life blew apart. From what she understood, Keera hadn't returned to dancing, and she was still quite withdrawn at school.

"Oma?" Lyla tugged at her hand.

"Ja, meine Mausi?" She probably should stop calling her a little mouse. The past few weeks, she'd come out of her shell.

"Do we really get to sit at the big table this year?"

"You sure do." It might be crowded, but she wanted the whole family at the table.

Myah came and gave her a hug. "Thank you for inviting us." She kissed Ida on both cheeks and then squeezed her hand. "I'm sorry we were late. Keera is having a hard day," she whispered.

"You're family now. I expect you here every holiday meal, cap-eesh?" She looked at Keera out of the corner of her eye and noticed she was holding hands with Lyla.

Myah nodded. "Thank you."

"All right." Ida clapped her hands together. "Sit. Doesn't mat-ter where. But children, you give the adults the big seats, *ja*?" She looked specifically at her grandsons.

In the hustle of the men and children sitting down while the girls helped Ida set the food out on the table, no one seemed to notice that Lyla and Keera were missing—no one other than Ida.

She heard their voices in the hallway and went to listen in. She pretended she was looking for something in the fridge.

"Are you okay?" Lyla asked Keera. "Why were you so late?"

"I didn't want to come." Keera's voice broke, and Ida had a feeling she was struggling not to cry. Tears came easily to the little one lately.

"Why not?"

"Just didn't. Things are different now."

Ida's heart sank.

"You don't miss your stepdad, do you?"

"Are you kidding me?" There was anger in Keera's voice. "You don't get it. No one does."

Ida needed to stop the conversation. This was something for adults to deal with, not little Lyla. But she stopped when she heard her granddaughter speak.

"I might not, but you're not alone. You're family now. Oma even said it. And today will be special. Trust me."

"Special? How?" Ida heard the spark of interest in Keera's voice and was proud of her little granddaughter.

"Oma always has a special surprise for us. I heard her talk to Opa a few days ago that this would be an extra special day." Her excited whisper did exactly what Ida thought Lyla meant it to do.

It gained Keera's attention.

"Really?"

Ida closed the fridge door and headed back to the table. "If you girls want any of these mashed potatoes, you'd better hurry up," she called out.

It made her heart happy to see a smile on Keera's face as the girls skipped together, hand in hand, toward the table.

That little girl's life wasn't going to be easy, and her heart would be broken over and over again, but she would be okay. The people at this table, those who loved her, would make sure of it.

ACKNOWLEDGMENTS

Writing is never a solitary voyage.

Thank you to my Super Aunt Deb (as she's affectionately known by my girls) for the late-night talks and text conversations, for answering all my questions, and for opening my eyes to the strength of those who dedicate their lives to protecting children. You are my hero, and without you, this book truly would not have been written.

Without the help of Lisa Snyder and Michael Bannerman, the details about how a school handles specific difficult situations would have been less true to life, though any errors made in this story are completely my own.

The journey I have taken throughout the creation of this story would not have been possible without the support of my readers, my SSS group, and my girlfriends who drag me away to the mountains to write and encourage me to imbibe Buttershots. To Melissa, for all that you do; to my amazing agent, Pamela Harty; and to the best editor in the world, Carmen Johnson. And finally, an apology to my family for getting lost in my story way too often and having to call for pizza delivery—although, honestly, if there's a choice between my cooking or ordering delivery, we all know who's the first to pick up the phone! I love you, and your support means the world to me!

ABOUT THE AUTHOR

Photo © 2013 Vanessa Pressacco Studios

With a passion for storytelling, Steena Holmes took her dream of being a full-time writer and made it a reality, writing her first novel while working as a receptionist. She won the National Indie Excellence Book Award in 2012 for her bestselling novel *Finding Emma* and has since continued to write stories that touch hearts. Holmes currently lives in Calgary, Alberta, with her husband, three daughters, and two dogs. When she's not traveling, she is either dreaming of a new adventure or writing about it.